Though rooted in historical fact, this narrative has been nourished by creative license. The personalities, characters and accompanying details are fabricated

Because there are many gaps in the historic documentation of Bass Reeves' life, this is a fictionalized narrative that does justice to the historical record, as well as pull Bass Reeves into the rank of other legendary characters of that time period.

The Adventures and Escapades
of
Bass Reeves

*African-American Lawman in the
Indian Territories*

Assunta Martin

The Adventures and Escapades
of
Bass Reeves

*African-American Lawman in the
Indian Territories*

Vanguard Press

A CIP catalogue record for this title is
available from the British Library.

ISBN 978 1 83794 009 7

*Vanguard Press is an imprint of
Pegasus Elliot Mackenzie Publishers Ltd.*
www.pegasuspublishers.com

First Published in 2024

**Vanguard Press
Sheraton House Castle Park
Cambridge England**

Printed & Bound in Great Britain

For my husband, Augie,
whose patience never wavered.
Thank you for your endless confidence and
encouragement.

I owe an immense debt to Dr. Art Burton, who introduced me to the heroic and remarkable character of Bass Reeves, as well as to the unsung role of African- Americans in the settlement and development of the Old West in the last quarter of the nineteenth century. His knowledge, enthusiasm and support for this narrative were my inspiration.

I also thank the many friends who encouraged me and were willing to read selected chapters and comment. A special shout-out to Dr. Marcella Sirhandi, whose warm and unflagging confidence in this venture was a constant motivation. Thanks also to Ken Bowman, Carrie Hulett, Leslie Yoshimura, Jess Davis, and Bob and Diane Graalman for their astute comments and support. All suggestions were much appreciated. Thank you to Keith Gotschall for introducing me to the Pony Express Museum.

I am grateful to everyone who took the time to help bring this narrative to life. This effort would not have come to fruition without their encouragement and interest in the story of this unsung hero.

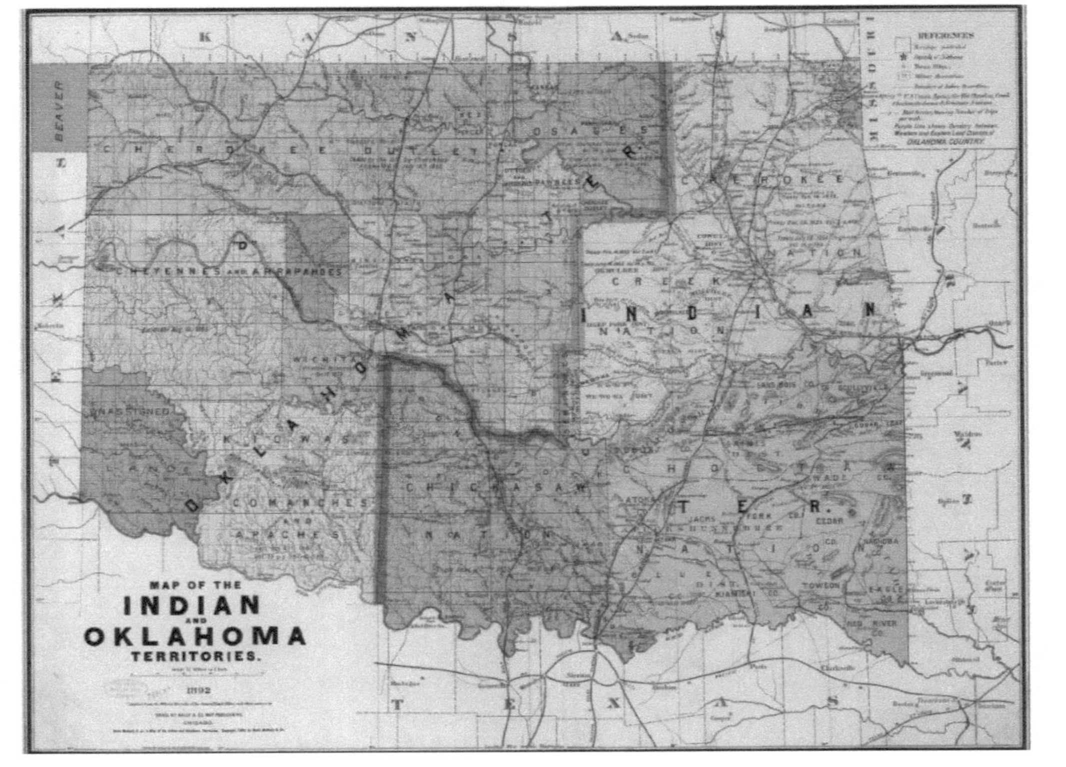

MAP OF THE
INDIAN
AND
OKLAHOMA
TERRITORIES.
1892
RAND, McNALLY & CO. MAP PUBLISHERS,
CHICAGO.
REFERENCES
OKLAHOMA COUNTRY.
KANSAS
MISSOURI
TEXAS
BEAVER
CHEROKEE OUTLET
CHEROKEE
CREEK
INDIAN NATION
OKLAHOMA
CHICKASAW NATION
CHEYENNES AND ARRAPAHOES
KIOWAS
COMANCHES AND APACHES
UNASSIGNED LANDS
WICHITA
OSAGES

Chapter 1

Escape

Vigorously massaging his throbbing right hand with his left, Bass stepped over the slumped body, carefully avoiding the small muddy puddle formed by a rivulet of blood trickling from his master's partially opened mouth. Calmly and surely, his prayer finally answered, Bass stretched his long muscular arm over the prostrate body of Colonel George, his master, and grabbed two Colt 45 pistols, the Henry Rifle, a small Derringer pocket pistol, and two boxes of cartridges from the top shelf of the cabinet next to the fireplace. He did not check for a pulse. Fully aware that a slave's assault of his master led straight to the hanging tree, Bass sprinted for the stables and swiftly saddled Magic, Bass's "own" steed used on hunts with the Colonel. In a run for his life, Bass headed for the Indian Territories, straight north to across the Red River.

Bass Reeves was born a slave in Colonel George's family in Arkansas and, at the age of eight, the colonel and his family moved to Texas, taking Bass with them. As he grew into manhood, Bass gained recognition and acclaim in the Texan household. His remarkable memory and quick intelligence, as well as his physical strength and wrestling skills, attracted the attention of his surly and arrogant master. George assigned Bass to be his personal body servant, an honored position in any slave holder's house. Bass often accompanied George as his assistant and companion on numerous hunting excursions. Plentiful wild game provided endless opportunities for Bass to master his marksmanship while he helped supply the ranch with a generous supply of rabbit, quail, turkey, and venison. George entrusted Bass to clean, polish, and oil the rifles in preparation for upcoming hunts. Also responsible for taking care of the master's race horses, Bass's enviable position in the household was respected and undisputed by the family and fellow slaves.

Although Bass was not even twenty years old, as the privileged manservant of the master, he enjoyed many more liberties than the other slaves in the household. He often witnessed the injustices suffered by others, who found themselves the unfortunate target of the master's immaturity and unfounded rages. The master's unpredictable anger could be triggered by the most meager of offenses. Just a few days before, Bass had witnessed the Colonel backhand the cook's young granddaughter on her chest for having forgotten to bring him his favorite orange marmalade for breakfast. Nothing angered Bass more than unfair bullying or abusive treatment of those who had to suffer the young master's insolence and impatience. The master, two decades older than Bass, concealed his secret fear of the clever manservant whose easygoing manner and expression of calm detachment unnerved him. Unable to assert himself around Bass, George vented his frustrations on the women and the youngest laborers on the small ranch. Shorter than Bass by at least six inches, Colonel George resented having to look up to Bass when talking to him. His closely set eyes, pursed thin lips, arched eyebrows, unkempt mustache, and sour demeanor did little to inspire confidence in his abilities or intellect. On the contrary, the colonel was known for his crudeness, laziness, and ill manners. Master George maintained despotic control of the household and both family members and slaves obeyed his whims and demands, eager to avoid one of his frequent outbursts of fury.

Bass was an excellent listener and keen observer. Even as a small child, he studied the ways the adults behaved and learned quickly how to endear himself with the master's family and with the seven other slaves. Riding into town with Master was a welcomed weekly rite and Bass noticed that the master was more at ease, laughing, and leaning in when sharing gossip with other moneyed men in town. *Quite a contrast to the brittle and harsh manner he brandishes with the maids, the cook, and the farmhands at home*, Bass wryly noted. Shrewd and cautious, Bass did not ask anyone about the curious and disturbing discrepancies in behavior he observed.

Two or three evenings a week, a stream of male guests visited the colonel's home to smoke, drink, and catch up on the latest gossip and news. When the guests, mostly other local plantation owners, lawyers, or affluent investors, came to visit Master George, Bass relished listening in to their conversations. Their boisterous exchanges, lubricated by ever more brandy or whiskey, unleashed exciting discussions about the "Indian Problem" or the open range in the west where cowboys and cattlemen freely rounded up long-horned cattle roaming the unfenced range.

Bass's assignment was to keep the fire tended and run errands if anything was needed. His presence was ignored by the rowdy men and Bass enjoyed that feeling, as if he were in some sort of magical disguise that protected him by keeping him invisible. As unremarkable as a familiar potted plant, he sat silently near the hearth, adding wood and stoking the burning logs. Every now and then, he would exchange the much-used spittoon for an empty one and slip back to his spot by the hearth. On occasions, particularly controversial topics would fuel the discussions late into the night and Bass would replace candles or trim the wicks of the oil lamps. As the evening wore on and the liquor flowed freely, unrestrained gestures increased and Bass was quick to mop up spills and replace drinks.

The conversations revealed much and served as Bass's informal education. Bass always tried to appear indifferent or bored with the animated conversations, but he soaked up every word and tried to make sense of what he was hearing. To witness the town elders—lawyers, ranchers, investors, and businessmen—carouse and shout out their opinions was stimulating entertainment for Bass. Their confidence and fearlessness at expressing opinions or outrage about perceived infractions was novel to Bass.

He intuited that similar vigorous expressions of anger by the folks he worked with and knew from the other ranches and farms would result in harsh and certain punishment. It was inconceivable that anyone laboring in his household, or any other, would express an opinion or ask a question about anything other than the manual chores at hand. Never discussed, but clearly understood, was that survival depended on the suppression of negative emotions and curiosity.

The most spirited topics were about troublesome or runaway slaves, the future of the stateless lands further west and north, and violent Indian wars and attacks on settlers. Another topic that always visibly animated the visitors was politics and there was unanimous support for the possible secession from the union by the southern slave-holding states. There was also talk about expanding the future confederacy by gaining control of the stateless lands. Some of the guests predicted that a war between the states was inevitable and, in five short years, they would be proven correct.

Of particular interest to Bass though were the stories told about the lawless Indian Territories north of the Red River that marked the boundary between Texas and the stateless territory, where thousands of Native Americans had been forcibly relocated by the federal government to free up more fertile land for the white settlers to farm in the southern states. Bass tried to imagine their lives after having left their ancestral lands and now sharing the dry and dusty unknown land with both past enemies and friends. That the Indian Nation was also a known and feared haven for fugitives sparked Bass's imagination. His young mind churned with unanswerable questions that he could ask no one. *What exactly did it mean to be a slave? What did it mean for his future? How many escaped slaves had made it to the Indian Nation and how did they survive there? Why was it so dangerous there? Did people survive by hunting? Was it true that some tribes had slaves? Were there any towns in the Indian Nation? How was the Indian Nation different from the state of Texas?*

George's good friend, Marcus Russel, was a frequent guest. A successful business man and investor, Russel was a retired military officer who had fought in the Second Seminole War with the colonel and had aided in the capture of Chief Osceola more than a decade before. His presence promised to add fiery sparks to the already rowdy exchanges. Bass was quick to realize that Marcus Russel held an honored position of respect on the guest list. Whenever he came galloping up to the house, Master George would have Bass unlock the tall rosewood cabinet that housed the best whiskeys, imported wines, and Virginian cigars purchased on his occasional trips to New Orleans. One evening, as he and the Colonel's friends shared a bottle of bourbon, Russel raged about two of his slaves, strong young men, whom he had recently purchased in New Orleans and were now thought to be hiding out in the brutal wild lands of the Indian Nation. Bass listened carefully as Russel shared the details of the price he had paid—an extravagant six hundred dollars each. Their successful escape was not only a significant economic loss, but it necessitated yet another long and arduous trip to New Orleans. Russel was incensed that neither state nor federal law officers would dare ride into the Indian Nation to shoot or capture the fugitives. The affluent investor did not hold the federal government in high regard and worked himself into an irrational lather when politics came up. That the Indian Nation was not under federal or state jurisdiction was incomprehensible to him, a travesty that obstructed prosperity and development. He often quoted President Andrew Jackson who, twenty-five years before, had taken up the cause for the relocation of the "savage Indians" west of the Mississippi River. Russel was fond of reminding the guests that Andrew Jackson, in his first annual message to Congress, asked the rhetorical question, *"What good man would prefer a country covered with forests and ranged by a few thousand savages to our extensive Republic, studded with cities, towns, and prosperous farms, embellished with all the improvements which art or industry can devise or execute, occupied by more than twelve million happy people, and filled with all the blessings of liberty, civilization, and religion?"* On the off chance that a few idealistic representatives might raise the pesky subject of fanciful and imagined rights for the tribes as accorded by previous treaties in the past, President Jackson clarified that removal of the indigenous tribes from the states would obviously *"enable those States to advance rapidly in population, wealth, and power,"* the most significant factor in the motive for relocating the tribes. *If only he were still alive,* Russel lamented, *he would remove the savages again, but this time he would herd them into the briny drink west of California.* Though Bass was not sure what "the briny drink west of California" was, he surmised that it was a cemetery for the inhabitants of the Indian Nation.

"The ungoverned stateless land is a refuge, a haven, for the lawless, and slaves who make it there are lost, valued property. Good land wasted on the uncivilized, hostile natives is madness... those treaties must be rescinded by the federal government! Who, in tarnation, gives a damn about those treaties and deals made by those chowderheads in the past? Our God-given destiny is to develop this vast land and profit from all of its natural bounty, our God-given destiny, damn it!" Russel thundered and cursed, pounding the mahogany table for emphasis. Encouraged by his attentive cigar-smoking audience, he poured another round of Kentucky bourbon for all and continued his tirade in the parlor of George's house. Heads all around nodded in somber agreement and the guests clinked glasses together in a toast of approval. A few raised their glasses to exuberant applause.

To Bass, quietly watching from the hearth, Russel reminded him of the neighbor's rabid dog that he had shot down the previous autumn when the poor hound's thrashing and foaming had caused great alarm to Master's children and their mother.

The men often complained and compared exorbitant prices they felt they had overpaid for their workers, their land, and their horses. In a short time, young Bass realized that the folks at home and at all the other estates—the cook, the maids, the farmhands—had been purchased and were owned by their masters. Previous comments and debates had roused Bass's suspicion, but now he finally understood the appalling truth. Like the land, house, and stable of fine horses, Bass and the people who worked the farm were the master's purchased and permanent property. *Property!* The revelation that he was owned by another man deeply disturbed and confused him and, the more he contemplated his position as a slave, the less he understood. *How was it possible for one man to be the possession of another man?* He could not bring himself to believe that obedience to the master and the unending hard work at Master George's plantation was his lot… that opportunity would never knock on his door, that he was doomed forever to be under the control and whims of a master. *Impossible*, he thought, *that is an unbearable future, there is no future for a slave, and I will not let this happen to me.* Galvanized by these defiant and mutinous thoughts, Bass determined that he would develop skills that would enhance his value as an 'asset' and might deliver him from slavery one day in the future when he was a grown man. Like a tiny snip of grass pushing up through the earth, a secret plan slowly began to unfurl in Bass's mind as he mulled over his situation. Bass confided in no one about the thoughts that began to swirl and seethe in his mind. He instinctively knew that even a whispered rumor among the household servants would assure him of severe punishment and foil his hope to escape forever.

Bass knew he had to proceed slowly and cautiously for the right time to carry out an exceedingly perilous plan that left no room for failure. As he deftly curried the master's prize horse, the circular pattern he used with the comb stirred old memories of childhood. As a very young boy, one of Bass's first daily chores was to fill buckets with water from a pond at the edge of the master's property. His job was to lug the full buckets back and pour them into a large barrel next to a newly planted orchard of peach trees near the house. This task entailed multiple trips back and forth. He would sometimes entertain himself by throwing pebbles or small rocks into the pond as he rested a few moments before hauling the next heavy load back to the orchard. The ever-widening ripples mesmerized him and, even though he threw the stone as far as he could, the ripples still danced and stretched across the pond until they gently lapped the grassy bank. The words spoken to him by the elderly Ivy, the kind and affectionate cook for the household, came to him… something about all deeds, like the stones cast in water, have a ripple effect… and something else she said had anchored itself in Bass… a stone thrown cannot be un-thrown. Bass pondered the mysteries of life. There was so much he didn't know or understand.

With his newly hatched but unformed plan, exhilaration grew. Bass strategized that gaining the confidence of his master was imperative. Young Bass determined he would become George's most reliable and dependable personal servant, a role he knew would entitle him to certain advantages that would benefit him when the moment came to escape. Though he knew he was smarter than the careless and arrogant Master George, he realized that Master George would have to believe the opposite, an easy task, since George was unusually susceptible to flattery and undeserved praise, and never doubted his own superiority to the slaves.

The privileged position Bass slyly maneuvered included such liberties as accompanying George on hunting forays and taking care of the highly valued race horses that George bought and sold. When Bass was about sixteen years old, he was given permission to name a new foal and train him for his own use when riding with George. Not unfamiliar with Bible stories, which were read to the household every Sunday evening by the mistress of the home, Bass wanted to name 'his' horse "Moses" after the African liberator of slaves in the ancient biblical days. When he mentioned this to Ivy, she stopped washing the pots, rinsed, and dried her hands before grabbing Bass by his shoulders and, looking hard into his eyes, said, *Listen to me, Bass. Don't use that name. No reason to raise suspicion that you might be looking for an escape someday. Everyone knows that Moses rescued the old-time slaves.* Bass wondered how Ivy knew what was so deeply buried in his heart. *I'll name him Magic... like the secret magic you and Ellie talk about late at night...*

Magic! And so, with Ivy's approving nod, the new colt was now named Magic.

Allowed to target practice, hunt, and handle the fine weapons that George collected was another significant indication of how successful Bass was in currying the Master's favor. The master bragged to his friends that it was uncanny how Bass always seemed to anticipate his needs. Never surly or defiant, Bass was the perfect slave, the master crowed, always obedient and willing to undertake any mission assigned to him.

On several occasions after a bountiful hunt, George would offer young Bass a glass of whisky but Bass always refused. Having often observed the potent effects a few glasses of the amber-colored fire water had on his master and his frequently visiting guests, Bass was well aware that alcohol was a devil's passkey that released the angry demons that apparently resided in every one of these visiting guests. George did not pressure Bass to drink. Perhaps he feared that the alcohol might bring trouble as it had for Marcus Russel a couple of years before. Russel came home one night to find one of his house servants passed out on the front porch and only learned the next day that the man had smuggled a bottle of whisky out of his master's locked liquor cabinet. After finishing off the jug, he turned the neighbor's horses loose and set the recently constructed barn on fire. The slave was never seen again and no one in the frightened Russel household dared to ask. Whispered rumors alleged that a few of the

community elders had swiftly arranged a necktie party in
the woods a few miles from Russel's home.

25

Chapter Two

Run to the Indian Nation

During the long, cold nights of winter and early spring, Master George, a habitual card player and gambler, would often call for young Bass to entertain him by joining him for several rowdy hours of poker. Like most slaves, Bass had never attended school or learned to read and write. He found the game stimulating and discovered quickly that, with minimal concentration, he could easily memorize all cards drawn and fallen. This skill assured him of winning most games, although he was prudent enough to allow his master more than an occasional win. Since Bass was not allowed to handle cash, the old ivory poker chips stored in a velvet-lined box on the granite mantel served as currency.

On that fated night, frustrated that he was unable to outwit an unschooled slave, George slyly eyed the nineteen-year-old Bass and connived to hide choice cards from a second deck beneath the deerskin that covered the inlaid table in front of the fireplace where they played nightly games. Reaching for the cigar cutter, George slid two aces under the soft hide. Little did Master George realize how this deceitful ploy would catapult his trusted manservant into a world of freedom and opportunity.

A barely visible twitch of George's eyebrow alerted Bass that the master was up to something devious. When Bass realized that George was cheating, it was impossible for him to subdue the dangerous flame of anger that crept steadily up his entire six-foot-plus frame. Leaping up from the table, Bass knocked over the heavy brass cuspidor and the three-legged stool that the master rested his pointed snakeskin boots on. Leaping up, Master George slipped in the spittoon spill of phlegm and tobacco muck, flailing wildly to grab one of the fireplace irons. As he lurched and stumbled toward the hearth, Bass slugged him; a powerful fist of destiny packed with a decade of repressed fury. Unexpectedly, George crashed unconscious to the floor, blood trickling slowly from his nose and mouth and rapidly pooling on the corner of the granite slab. The passionate rage ignited by the master's attempted deception vanished abruptly, and an unfamiliar thrill born of sudden liberty electrified Bass. Strangely, Bass felt no fear—only an urgency to grab what he needed, saddle Magic, and get as far as possible from the colonel's household before anyone was alerted.

As he raced Magic through the moonlit brush, following a well-concealed trail of preceding fugitives, Bass wondered why he had delayed so long in making his escape. Though Colonel George's spread was only twenty-odd miles from the southern border of the Indian Territories, those twenty perilous miles were the difference between life and death and seemed to stretch into a distance ten times the geographic reality. The broad and meandering Red River that snaked lazily between Texas and the lawless Indian Nation lay ahead of him. As Bass rounded a thicket of scraggly cedar trees and the river rose into sight, he saw a small group of men, their ponies silhouetted in the dim glow of a campfire. Gentle strumming of a stringed instrument echoed across the water. The men could have been cattle drovers, outlaws, travelers heading west, or campers noodling for channel catfish. Taking no chances on an unpleasant encounter, Bass swiftly veered clear of the campsite, steering Magic east and out of sight of the group.

The light of the full moon sparkling on the sandbars pointed out the route Bass should take. Spring thunderstorms that would swell the treacherous waters and choke them with debris were yet to come. Bass started humming and smiled at the fortunate timing as he gently urged his beloved horse, now truly his own horse, across the chilly, but placid river. When Magic bobbed and nodded his head as he trotted across a sand bar, Bass felt with absolute clarity that Magic understood the utter graveness of their situation. Bass rubbed his neck and whispered in his ear the name he had given the baby colt a few years earlier. Though not a believer in ritual, unlike his mistress and some of the other household members, Bass did believe powerful spiritual and unseen supernatural forces guided individuals through their lives. The Sunday evening Bible readings by the mistress of the household rarely excited him as much as the ancient stories of a mysterious and magical world retold time and again by his fellow slaves, and particularly by the wise cook, Ivy. In his young mind, all stories intertwined, offering not only wisdom but also caution and comfort as well. He cautiously attributed his successful escape, in part, to the auspicious name he had given his horse, a word inspired by the tales Ivy whispered late at night to her fellow slaves.

Let's go! Magic, Magic, Magic, he repeated as they splashed through the shallow water to the other side of the river that bordered the Indian Nation. Bass had the curious thought that he and Magic, now fellow fugitives and no longer the valued possessions of Master, seemed to share an unspoken bond. Like loyal brothers, they would depend on each other for survival as they journeyed together toward the unknown future. The stone was thrown; the ripples were circling and expanding. Bass and Magic galloped ever faster into an uncertain future.

Bass, now in the ungoverned lands, breathed easier and dismounted. With no plan or knowledge of the layout of the territories, he did not feel safe and, after giving Magic a brief rest and a rubdown, Bass charged on for another hour, knowing that every mile further north lessened the chance of being tracked down or shot by eager slave hunters hoping for a sizable reward from the master's family for his capture.

The passage of the Fugitive Slave Act six years before in 1850 had emboldened many vigilantes to track and hunt down escaped slaves to return them to their owners in exchange for compensation. Bass had heard stories of greedy or foolhardy slave catchers who crossed the Red River in pursuit of escapees. The vigilantes hovered near the sandy bank, patrolling the ridge, and watched for signs of activity, but deep fear judiciously prevented them from venturing further. The rewards offered were never generous enough to risk their own lives in the anarchic Indian Nation, the favored name used by the neighboring states. The few stubborn bounty hunters who ignored warnings and dared to advance a few miles north of the Red River did so at their own peril and some never returned.

The gruesome stories about justice meted out to white intruders, bounty chasers, and squatters in the Indian Nation were enough to discourage all but the most blustering of slave hunters. On the north bank of the river, it was not unusual to see a dead cottonwood or a spiny locust tree festooned with sun-bleached animal skulls hanging from the limbs, an ominous warning to any who dared delve deeper into the stateless land. Grotesque mobiles made of teeth and finger bones clicked and rattled from the skeletal branches in the breeze. No one lingered at the macabre sight long enough to count the number of human skulls decorated with feathers and strangely painted signs that dangled from the leafless branches.

After checking his surroundings carefully, Bass stopped near a shallow creek edged with birch trees and rough brush. Under a canopy of glittering stars and the floating silent moon, he drifted into a heavy sleep, waking just before dawn. The thin clouds that veiled the full moon evaporated as a halo of light fringed the eastern horizon. Bass did not know why the melancholy cooing of unseen mourning doves so moved him that morning. Rested, but hungry, Bass saddled up Magic and pushed onward, desiring only to flee deeper and deeper into the Indian lands. Bass contemplated his new status as a fugitive slave as he wound his way north through the wooded lands of the Choctaw, the first of the eastern tribes to be relocated to the Indian Territories.

Originally from Mississippi and Alabama, the Treaty of Dancing Rabbit Creek had ceded the land that Bass Reeves rode through to the Choctaws twenty-six years earlier in 1830. With no options, the survivors of the forced march united in their effort to rebuild the once flourishing communities that had prospered so well in Mississippi. Relocated to the southeastern corner of the Indian Nation, the Choctaw citizens worked hard in an ultimately futile effort to co-exist with the Christian missionaries and the continually encroaching pioneers and squatters in the Territories. They cleared land to farm, built log cabins and schools, and later helped the early Presbyterian advocates build one of the first stone churches in the Choctaw Nation. Rather than be annihilated, the Choctaw wanted to understand the white culture and welcomed the Christian proselytizers who would educate and help acculturate their children by teaching them English. Not willing to abandon their forefathers' spiritual beliefs, many Choctaw families cautiously integrated some of the new theology being taught. On the southern border of the Indian Territories, along the Red River, wealthier Choctaws managed small plantations and owned slaves who eventually assimilated into the community as they learned the language and absorbed the culture. The slaves of the Choctaws did menial labor, helped with the farming and building, and were generally treated as part of the clan, albeit lower in status than full-blood tribal members. The mostly benign relationship between the slave laborers and their owners encouraged mutual assimilation.

It was not unusual for fugitive slaves to marry eventually within the tribe and have families of their own, thereby increasing the population and strength of the community. Familiar only with white men who owned slaves, Bass mused that, because the Choctaws came from two of the harshest slave states, their culture must have adopted the slave owner mentality of the white plantation owner, and that the wealthier Choctaws must have also endorsed the belief that Bass's people were inferior and so could be exploited without consequence. Bass calmly puzzled over this new mystery of the social dynamic that he could not understand.

By now, Colonel George and the community back in Texas would be furiously searching for him. Bass hoped for forgiveness from the household slaves whom he knew would be mercilessly interrogated and probably punished for his assault on Master George, the theft of valuable weapons, and his escape with Magic.

Bass was sure that a reward for returning Magic, not a prized racehorse, would be no incentive for the slave hunters. Without a shadow of regret or remorse for his assault on Master George, Bass wondered briefly if he had killed Master George or only knocked him unconscious. If the Colonel died by his fist, Bass knew that the search for the killer would be lengthy and thorough, drastically diminishing his chances of eluding the law.

Despite Bass's conflicted feelings about the Choctaws as he galloped through their lands, the people he met as he rode north were hospitable, offering him simple meals and pointing out trails to follow on his winding journey north. The unexpected camaraderie and pleasantness among the Choctaw families and their slaves, treated like friends, or even family members, surprised Bass. Small log cabins dotted the land but there was no sign of a village. A rustic trading post at a fork on the trail was a welcome sight for Bass and he stocked up on basic supplies in exchange for several skinned rabbits and two wild turkeys he had shot earlier in the day. Game was abundant and Bass's hunting prowess kept him well-fed and strong and served as the currency he needed for trade.

Bass continued to follow the Choctaw trail in a north-easterly direction. The further he embedded himself in the Indian Nation, the safer he felt. He experienced no malice from the tribal communities, contrary to the rant-filled stories Master George and his cronies shared. On the contrary, he felt warmly welcomed and even admired. Confidence grew as he continued. *I think I can survive in the Territories*, Bass realized with a growing sense of elation and strength.

No one could predict the extraordinary events that would sabotage even the best of preparations in the explosively changing times. Already alarming discussions and passionate arguments about hostilities between the Northern and the Southern states were punctuated with whispers of secession from the union—the country might be divided into two nations! The dire forecasts by pessimistic citizens that a civil war was inevitable came true a few years later.

Still wanting to get as far north of the Texas border, Bass reasoned that his safest refuge would be beyond the Ouachita Mountains further north toward the Cherokee and Creek lands. A young Choctaw brave sketched a map, marking out a well-traveled trail on a piece of hide that would lead Bass through the rough hills and pine forests. Bass was assured that a vast lacework of caves throughout the San Bois hills and mountains would offer protection and shelter but was warned to be on constant alert for bandits and robbers who routinely retreated to the craggy hills to stash their ill-gotten loot in well-concealed crannies and crevices. The desperados kept their eyes peeled for any suspicious transients riding the rocky and hilly trails. Lingering in the rugged mountains or cave exploration was ill-advised.

Bass was grateful to the eager scout, who, impressed with Bass's quick skill and interest in Choctaw vocabulary, coupled with his calm and composed manner, impulsively offered to ride with Bass across the San Bois region and on to the North Fork of the Canadian River. Pleased to have a companion who generously shared invaluable tips and information, the two traveled onward together for more than a week. Bass's new friend explained that his name, Tuska-homa, meant Red Warrior, an auspicious and ancient name that was given to him by his great uncle who had fought in countless battles in the past and had survived the relocation journey. That someday the Indian Nation would become a state of the union with the Choctaw name of Oklahoma, Red People, was unimaginable.

Tuska-homa agreed that Bass would find loyal protection as a fugitive with the Creeks. Not only was it extremely unlikely that Bass would ever be tracked so far north, but he could count on a welcoming community of others who had also suffered mistreatment by southern land grabbers and plantation owners. The shared experience of victimization and treachery would assure both protection and support. This was, of course, a powerful bond that Bass shared with all of the tribal communities.

Bass had also heard of a famous Creek chief of the Upper Creeks, and Tuska-homa spoke with great reverence about the renowned and fearless chief of the Creeks, Opothleyhola, the son of a European man and a Creek mother. He was a skilled orator, a famed warrior in the first two Seminole wars, and, in his later years, known for his tireless efforts to negotiate with the Indian Agents and the federal government. He was chosen to be the representative in the National Council as head chief in dealing with the government about the loss of their homelands, the continuing encroachment of settlers, and the broken treaties and agreements. Bass felt magnetically drawn to the powerful man who had committed his life to save his people and preserve their rights.

The speed with which Bass's new circumstances had erupted had necessarily negated any well-thought-out plan, other than fleeing to the Territories to save his life. Now Bass was determined to meet the fearsome and courageous warrior whose wise advice might offer guidance and friendship. Bass had adopted a mantra—perhaps from Sunday evening Bible readings by the mistress, or maybe from Ivy—that encouraged him to be patient. *Everything will unfold in its own time*, Bass whispered to Magic. Magic bobbed his head and whinnied in agreement.

Tuska-homa's loyalty to the fugitive from Texas was secured forever when Bass saved his life as they rode the twisting, rocky trail. After riding a few hours the first morning, they stopped for a longer break on one of the bluffs overhanging a densely treed valley. As they prepared to roast the rabbit snagged earlier in the morning, Tuska-homa gathered small dry twigs and grass to start the fire. Just as he crouched low and leaned across a slab of rock, Bass saw a flick, a glint, a flash of something moving on the rock to the left of Tuska-homa's shoulder. A timber rattlesnake camouflaged against the dun-colored rocks slowly unwound itself. Multicolored scales pulsed and glinted in the sunlight. The low hum that increased in loudness became a frantic buzzing, a sound that Bass was all too familiar with. The four-foot-long rattlesnake was about to strike Tuska-homa's neck, only inches away. Stretched out flat on his stomach, the young brave was tugging and yanking on a stubbornly rooted dry bush and did not hear the warning. Quicker than the viper, Bass leveled his revolver and, with one shot, killed the venomous reptile. At the sound of the unexpected pistol shot a few feet from him, Tuska-homa jerked back, leaped up, and stared at Bass with fear and disbelief. *Was this seemingly friendly stranger going to murder him in the remote hills? Could his intuition have been so misguided?* Bass smiled and pointed to the writhing bisected snake. Relief surged through him as he skillfully removed the head, fangs and the rattler and peeled the iridescent skin off the serpent to preserve for later use. Grilled rattlesnake steak was added to the meal's already tasty menu.

Tuska-homa, eternally grateful to Bass, knew that, without a doubt, the venomous rattler's poisonous blow on his neck would have ended his life. Traveling on, the two finally reached the North Fork of the Canadian River. Before separating, Bass and Tuska-homa shared a pipe of willow bark and sumac to seal their young but strong friendship. As a parting gift, Tuska-homa gave Bass a deerskin pouch with a curious central design artfully decorated in black and white seed beads. A few years later, in an attempt to escape the violence of the War Between the States, Tuska-homa, the Red Warrior, would head north to search for Bass in the Creek Nation and volunteer to work with him.

On the north side of the Canadian River, Bass set up a rudimentary camp. It was mid-spring. The fields and woods vibrated and swelled with renewed life. The crisp cool days, sporadic rain showers, and the fresh greening of the trees and the grass invigorated Bass. No longer fearing slave chasers, Bass calmly weighed his future. His first goal was to meet Chief Opothleyhola.

Early spring rains further north had washed detritus into the creeks, clogging them with fallen brush and scree. Crossing more rivers and weaving northeast, Bass came to the wide and rain-swollen Arkansas River. Bass welcomed the advice shared by locals and travelers who directed each other to the best spots to ford the river and warned about treacherously deep channels to be avoided. Stories of drownings and jettisoned possessions circulated among the travelers and hunters. The river bed, fed by capsized wagons and trunks, was rich with lost treasures buried in the thick sediment. Small wood crosses and the names of unfortunates sucked away by the swift rapids and turbulent undercurrents were carved out in the trunks of trees bordering the river. Bass determined then and there that he would learn how to swim in the future, a necessary skill that may save his life one day, or help him save another's.

Small settlements, made up of a few log cabins, were scattered along the banks. Roughly constructed trading posts peppered the area. Bass and Magic continued the difficult journey without major mishap. Within a short time, Bass, always sharply discerning, was able to identify tribal affiliation by clothing and language. Creeks, Cherokees, Potawatomi, Shawnees, fur trappers, and traders plied their goods and bantered with Bass who had never before enjoyed the confidence, friendliness, or social recognition of mingling with such a diverse community. That he was obviously an escaped slave, a fugitive on the run, stirred no alarm or interest in the people he met now. Secrets were safely stashed and no one asked prying questions. When strangers crossed paths, trust was determined by acute observation and insightful intuition because no one doubted that survival in the wild lands depended on mutual cooperation.

Chapter 3

Life and Education in the Indian Nation

When Bass finally met the famous Chief of the Upper Muskogee Creeks, he was not disappointed. Chief Opothleyhola was born near the end of the eighteenth century. In his mid-sixties, he was vigorous, articulate, and intelligent. He welcomed Bass warmly and invited him to consider settling in the lands assigned to the Creek Nation in the northeastern section of the Indian Nation, just south of the land designated for the Cherokee people. Unused to such immediate acceptance, Bass was characteristically wary, though an unfamiliar and humbling feeling of gratefulness and optimism flooded through him. He had Tuska-homa to thank for telling him about the chief. The tales the older chief narrated were enlightening and Bass learned about intra-tribal wars and the split between the Upper and the Lower Creeks. He would learn just how divisive the split would become when the brutality of the war between the southern and the northern states spilled into the Indian Nation a few years later.

The friendships and alliances that Bass forged during the years he lived with the Creeks and his many experiences with the neighboring Cherokees would give him unrivaled skills in speaking tribal languages, understanding multiple dialects, a thorough knowledge of the topography of the Indian Territories, and, as a bonus, an abundance of clever tricks of deception and survival that would be of infallible benefit in the future. Bass settled in a Creek area that later would grow into the town of Muskogee. His horse riding skills, love of animals, and knowledge of both English and weaponry were impressive, gaining him fame and trust. Bass exhibited a much-admired expertise for training dogs and breaking in horses. Hardworking and always ready to help, Bass soon became a teacher of the ways and language of the white men and an eager and respectful student of the native cultures.

Handsome, self-disciplined, and talented, many unmarried women, charmed by him, vied for his attention. Bass, still very aware of being an escaped slave, was reserved and, though he engaged in frivolous banter with flirtatious young women, it was not the right time for him, he thought, to settle into a life of routine and responsibilities. It was unusual for a young man to delay marriage and family, but Bass was restless and content to remain single. Bass, free from the yoke of slavery, reveled in his new-found liberty and welcomed the as-yet, unrevealed options his new life offered.

The Indian Removal Act passed in 1830 under President Andrew Jackson, who was no friend of the indigenous people, forced the Cherokee, Seminole, Creek, Chickasaw, and Choctaw tribes, known as The Five

Civilized Tribes, to sell at a low price or relinquish their bountiful eastern lands to the government in a devil's bargain. Bass had often heard that fiery topic discussed when he was a slave in Texas. His mind flashed back to the hotheaded Marcus Russel whose hero was President Jackson. Now he was hearing stories from both victims and their descendants about the brutal removal and relocations of the ruthless policies. Master George and his circle never mentioned the hardship, deaths, or cruelty of the forced marches of the tribes.

By 1838, President Van Buren, heavily pressured by zealous Southern settlers wanting to explore newly discovered gold deposits in Georgia on Cherokee land and plantation owners who lusted for more of the fertile land to expand the cotton industry, angrily demanded a solution. The remaining seventeen thousand Cherokee men, women, and children were rounded up, corralled in stockades, and escorted on a forced march west to the Indian Nation by an armed militia of seven thousand troops. Horses and other livestock were confiscated as their homes were ransacked and plundered. The communal wealth of the tribal community vanished in seconds. Not allowed to gather any belongings or clothing, the tribe was reduced to a broken and humiliated mass, huddled together in cattle stockades until everyone was rounded up before the cruel trek began.

Belligerent soldiers riding alongside, kept their weapons loaded, cocked, and aimed during the mandatory and brutal exodus. Any excuse to flex the trigger finger was welcomed without a second thought. Those who lagged back or tried to escape were shot on the spot and left to the elements. There was no mercy or patience for the elderly or the children. The bitter cold, exhaustion, disease, lack of food, water, warm clothing, and foot wear took a devastating toll. More than four thousand Cherokee men, women, and children died on the cruel and intentionally circuitous and lengthy trails to the lands west of the Mississippi River, a seemingly vast and infertile wasteland. Weather in all of its extremes seemed to gravitate toward the barren land. Howling, frigid winds and ice storms swept through the prairies during winter and, in the summer, tornadoes, lightning strikes, hot winds, and blasting temperatures fueled blazing infernos that raced through the flat grasslands. Those strong enough to survive the yearlong cruel trek of more than a thousand miles were abandoned in the ungoverned land and many died soon after of disease or starvation. This was the last of the inhumanly enforced exoduses of the indigenous people to the new "Indian Nation."

Bass's education about history was greatly expanded and enlightened by Chief Opothleyhola who gladly mentored his young admirer. Bass learned that under the Indian Removal Acts President Jackson signed into law, more than one hundred thousand people were violently uprooted and effectively banished to the Indian Nation between the years of 1830 to 1838. The Choctaws were the first of the Indian nations to be cruelly marched, many bound in chains, to the stateless territory west of the

Mississippi. The tribal name for President Jackson was Sharp Knife, a fitting name for the man who was responsible for stabbing the indigenous people in the back as he violently severed off their homeland to benefit the greed-driven plantation owners.

Bass Reeves was a welcomed member of the tribal communities, sharing a common history of treacherous dealings with wealthy white Southerners. His expert horsemanship, coupled with his skillful use of guns, continued to achieve mythic proportion among his tribal friends. It was said he could shoot the eye of a fly on the ear of a horse at five hundred yards using either hand. Bass's ambidexterity attracted admirers and he was often pressed to demonstrate the ease and speed of his marksmen skills, confidently and accurately firing his six-shooter as he switched back and forth from left to right hand and back again without ever missing the target. His reputation and popularity began to spread among the tribal communities. Unlike many others hiding out in the lawless lands, Bass easily mastered the Creek and Seminole languages, thereby gaining the respect and admiration of people both inside and outside of the Indian Nation. Later, Bass would become a trusted ally for the besieged tribes who would side with the Union when war was officially declared.

The years in the wild lands, fighting and protecting the people he had grown to know so well, and his loyal friendships with Opothleyahola and other tribal leaders, fostered the respect, loyalty, and honesty that would forever color Bass's future. During those years, Bass earned the praise and enduring friendship of Minewa, a grandson of the tribal shaman, who later served as a trusted companion and scout for Bass. The skills that saved Bass's life in dire times: locating water, starting a fire, whisper walking, using sign language, and tracking forest animals and humans were all invaluable secrets passed on to him by Minewa. By mastering the imitation of distinctive cries of the wild pheasant, the shrieks of the red-tailed hawks, the hoots of the screech owl, and the mournful coo of the doves, Bass learned the covert language by which tribal members communicated with each other when circumstances necessitated stealth or caution. Bass remembered the pledge he made to himself on the journey north and Minewa taught Bass to swim, first in a small lake, and then, the more challenging task of navigating across a river despite rough rapids or strong currents.

Both Minewa and Bass were patient and humorous young men who enjoyed trying to outwit each other. Like close brothers, they shared their particular expertise and knowledge with each other. Not only did Bass help Minewa improve his shooting skills and teach him English, but he also introduced him to the peculiar customs of the white men's culture. Minewa taught Bass how to ride without a saddle and a few clever riding tricks and, within a short time, Bass, despite his six-foot-plus frame, could create the illusion, when observed from a distance, that he was shorter than he was, a strategy that would prove useful in the future when Bass was on the hunt for outlaws and did not want his famed height to betray his identity.

The humiliating defeat and betrayals that resulted in the compulsory migration of the Cherokee Nation on the Trail of Tears, only a little more than two decades before, had not faded from living memory. It was common knowledge among the tribal communities that the few thousand Choctaws and Cherokees, who had opted to remain in their homelands during the first removal, had suffered mightily from ill-treatment and blind prejudice as legislated by the state. The promises of allotments and property agreements made stateside were not enforced and those who had refused to leave were now destitute and barely able to survive as sharecroppers on what had once been their own land. The thriving communities and farms that had flourished for generations were sold or given away in lotteries to the white settlers and the remaining members of the tribe suffered further discrimination, violence, and abject humiliation at the hands of the settlers and the state government.

Chapter 4

War Between the States Erupts

Only a month after the election of President Lincoln in 1861, civil war broke out. Less than three months later, Congress passed the Homestead Act, signed a year later by President Abraham Lincoln. These two events, both of great significance, shaped the direction and growth of the young United States. The passage of the Homestead Act was celebrated by hundreds of thousands of people who were eager to own land, build towns, farm and move on with the development of the vast lands out west. With the secession of the southern states, the controversial bill was passed, blazing a trail to land ownership and accelerating western expansion.

Twenty-four years after the forced removal of the last tribes east of the Mississippi to the unwanted lands now designated as the Indian Nation, the Civil War between the Union and the Confederate States exploded. Creeks, Seminoles, Choctaws, Chickasaw, and Cherokees who had been relocated were now pressured by southern states to join the Confederacy. The onset of the Civil War revived past intertribal hostilities and the past twenty years of greater mutual cooperation eroded swiftly. Since many of the uprooted tribes had both past alliances and bitter hostilities with the South, tension and conflicted loyalties ran amok. Many of the more affluent tribal communities accepted slavery; however, if the Southern states seceded from the union, the tribes within the reserved land would surely suffer since all existing treaties and agreements were with the federal government.

The tribes bitterly blamed the South for the Indian Removal Acts of the past which had legalized the blatant plunder and theft of their homelands. No financial compensation could equal the loss of their ancestral lands and lifestyle. Arguments and violent skirmishes among the tribes increased and, those who felt abandoned by the federal government and afraid that the nation was about to splinter, looked to their Indian Agents for guidance. Many of the agents were from southern states and, as staunch advocates of the current politics of the Confederacy, urged the conflicted people to fight against the Union. Pressure mounted daily. Agents, fully confident that victory would fall to the Confederates, made wild and generous promises they never expected to honor about the future role and prosperity of the native tribes.

As the War Between the States intensified, Native Americans in the Territories continued to be pressured to support the southern cause, stirring passionate debate as agitators fueled past hostilities among the tribes. When the federal armies abandoned the forts in the Indian Territories, the Confederate Army moved in quickly and, within a short time, all Five Civilized Tribes (a term used by the government to distinguish those tribes that would willingly assimilate from other 'wild and savage' tribes) were compelled to sign treaties with the Confederacy. Intertribal feuding over this issue interrupted all attempts to settle peacefully in the new land. Many tribal chiefs felt loyalty to the Union and had little trust in the motives and ambitions of the South. Their lack of trust rested in their own tribal removals and subsequent loss of ancestral lands. Their culture, language, and "assigned" property were surely to be wiped out next. The vision of a prosperous and free Indian Nation inhabited by diverse tribes whose destinies were under their own command was proving to be a rapidly fading illusion harbored now by only the hopeful and the naïve. With the erosion of trust and hope, more violence fueled by fear spread throughout the Indian Nations. Tribes were no less conflicted in allegiance than were the European immigrant settlers, pioneers, and squatters throughout the nation.

Ideology played a lesser role in the rising class of opulent tycoons whose overriding interest was to be on the side of the victors so they could continue to profit abundantly in the development of the new nation. Prosperous businessmen or investors were primarily concerned with the adverse economic impact the War Between the States would have, as any war threatened to delay progress in the ongoing and long-planned development of a transcontinental railroad network and further explorations to locate and develop the highly valued resources of oil, natural gas, and precious metals.

Investors were intrigued by the new drilling techniques used with the first commercial oil well in Pennsylvania. Rumors of another gold rush, this time in the state of Georgia, only intensified the violent competition to gain control of resources and opportunities in the rapidly developing new nation.

The Creek Nation was split asunder, with the majority of the tribe siding with the Confederates. The Chief of the Upper Creek Nation of the Muscogee District, Chief Opothleyahola, felt no loyalty to the southern states and refused to join the Confederacy. He remained steadfastly faithful and unwavering in his allegiance to the Union and Bass unhesitatingly sided with his mentor and friend, whose tribe had been forced by the Indian Removal Act to abandon the eastern woodlands decades before and start a new life in the empty lands west of the Mississippi River. Chief Opothleyahola encouraged his people to adhere to the ancient customs and traditional lifestyle of the Creeks despite the merciless and fierce war that was ripping families apart and severing tribal fealty.

Like the Choctaw and other tribes forced to move to the Indian Nation, the Creek communities had adapted to the harsh new life and cultivated fields, built log cabins, opened business of trade, and provided education for their youth. Adapting and cooperating with the ever-increasing intrusion of squatters, missionaries, federal officials and Indian Agents were matters of survival and often of mutual benefit for all, but Opothleyhola, or "Laughing Fox" as he was known by his people, was a tireless supporter of his culture and the ways of the past. His entire life had been guided by his proud devotion to the preservation of the Creek identity and customs, and a blind trust that justice and fairness would prevail for his people.

Known for his masterful oratory skills and diplomatic efforts over decades to work with the federal government, Opothleyhola dispatched a message to President Lincoln asking for help and quickly received a response. He was assured that, as loyalists to the Union, his people would find protection and aid in Kansas at Fort Row across the northern border of the Territories. A large group of Seminoles and others who shared a common distrust and fear of the Confederate forces joined the terrified and fleeing population. Freedmen, escaped slaves, and locals from other tribes joined in yet another great diaspora, known as The Trail of Blood on Ice.

A group of humiliated Choctaws, previously abandoned in Georgia, also joined those desperate to escape conscription by the Confederates, and among those was a brother of Tuska-homa, Bass's first friend in the Indian Nation. Tuska-homa traveled with his brother and together they fled north following the same trails he had guided Bass through in the San Bois Mountains. After making it safely across the Canadian River, they galloped onwards following the banks of the northern bank of the Arkansas River into the Cherokee nation. It was only then that he started to search for Bass. Bass had not forgotten Tuska-homa and had been happily surprised to hear from one of the Lighthorse Police that a Choctaw man named

Red Warrior was searching for him and had recently camped in the Cherokee Nation. Within ten days, the two men joyfully reunited and celebrated the steadfastness of their friendship. They had much to catch up on and Bass promised that Tuska-homa would soon meet his much-admired hero, Chief Opothleyahola.

The Cherokee Nation and other tribes who had allied with the Confederacy were under command to stop the fleeing Creeks. Bass assured Chief Opothleyahola that the divisiveness that churned through the Cherokee Nation would render the majority of them incapable of attacking the fleeing refugees. As usual, the perceptive intelligence of Bass Reeves was prescient. The general suspicion of their new southern allies, who had, after all, forced them to leave their beloved homeland, increased as the large Cherokee regiment drew closer to the hidden camp of the Creeks. Just as confrontation appeared imminent, the regiment scattered, and many deserted the Rebel forces to band with Opothleyahola and his followers.

With the promise of help and asylum by President Lincoln, Opothleyahola and five thousand loyal followers retreated north in the bitter winter of 1861 to Kansas in yet another perilous and desperate trek, enduring three ferocious battles with Confederate soldiers within five weeks. The last of the three battles, the Battle of Chustenahlah, ended with a victory for the Confederate troops. The victors took possession of hundreds of cattle, five hundred horses, captured one hundred-and-twenty-five women, killed two hundred-and-fifty men, and wildly looted everything of value. When the refugees were again attacked by a disparate group of warriors from scattered tribes allied with the enemy and Chief Opothleyahola lost another fifteen men, he gave up the fight, fleeing with the survivors north to Fort Row in desperate need of the pledged federal support by President Lincoln.

Tuska-homa did not hesitate to join Bass and his neighbor, Jackson Longarm, on the trek to Kansas. Accompanying the ragged and miserable refugees for several days, the three men provided cover and hunted game for the starving people. Game was scarce in the land blanketed with ice and snow and the three partners trapped and shot what they could to help feed the weakened, displaced men, women, and children. Heavily iced branches crashed down, blocking the trail, adding further challenges as the refugees trudged north to presumed safety. Tuska-homa, Jackson, and Bass cleared the trail ahead in an effort to expedite the exodus. Riding alongside Opothleyahola for much of the way to the northern border of the Territories, Bass's allegiance and help to the tribe would be rewarded in the years to come.

Never had Bass seen such a heart-rending sight as this tragic caravan of men, women, and children demoralized by recent defeats in three bloody battles en route. Assaulted by the icy winter winds as they made their way through the difficult terrain, was as devastating a journey as the Trail of Tears forced marches decades before that Bass had heard so often about from tribal elders.

Finally, the ruined, half-naked hordes of people on foot, horses, and in broken-down wagons reached the border of the Indian Territories and reassembled in Kansas on the Verdigris River. The tattered threadbare clothing and minimal supplies could not shield the ten thousand poorly prepared people from the fierce and unforgiving weather. With neither enough food nor moccasins, nor adequate shelter or protection, they suffered heavy losses, losing more than two thousand horses and hundreds of followers. The refugees had never suspected that the conditions at Fort Row would be so horrendous; lacking medical supplies, food, blankets, and winter clothing. William Coffin, assigned as regional superintendent, was able to arrange only for minimal supplies from the promised federal aid, and he and his son donated their own salaries to help feed the multitude of starving people. Lack of medical assistants, nurses, doctors, or basic medicines resulted in inexpert amputations for many of those who suffered from severe frostbite. Unable to provide adequate care, blankets, clothing, or basic necessities, the refugees who had survived the long and challenging exodus, were transferred to Fort Belmont, yet another fort equally unprepared to feed and clothe the destitute and miserable asylum seekers. Only the hardiest individuals survived, as starvation and exposure claimed the old, weak, young, and the ill. Any remaining morale was crushed when the tribe's heroic and defiant leader, Chief Opothleyahola, died the following year in the refugee camp near the Sac and Fox Indian Agency in Quenemo, Kansas. That the fearless warrior who had fought in endless wars and battles to save his people died such an inglorious death, was a shameful travesty too heavy to shoulder.

Although the Indian Territories remained relatively free of the raging battles fought in the southern states, the people who lived in the reserved lands suffered enormously. The prosperity that the Choctaws, Creeks, and Cherokees had once enjoyed, vanished in the flames of a war driven by greed, economics, and politics. Torched farms, looted businesses, massacres, rampant horse and cattle theft, random lynchings, and indiscriminate slaughter of families were chilling testimonies of the madness that raged through the unassimilated nation. Native Americans who sided with either the Confederate or the Union forces found themselves under siege. In 1862, when the Confederate Indian agent and two of his men assigned to the Tonkawa tribal community were killed by a band of pro-Union tribal warriors, the fleeing Tonkawa community was massacred. The loss of the chiefs and most of the population disseminated the tribe and those who survived lived in abject poverty on the outskirts of Fort Belknap in Texas. Twenty-two years later, the small band of survivors and their descendants were relocated back to Oklahoma.

In the vast stateless lands out west, wars and battles between the native people and local militias raged. Threatened and forced to align themselves in the civil war between the states, ancient intertribal hostilities were stoked and deadly skirmishes among warring tribal bands flared. There were few in the Indian Nation who had not heard about the brutal massacre at Sand Creek in the bordering Colorado Territories, where a village of a few hundred unsuspecting Cheyenne and Arapahos, mostly women and children, were murdered by six hundred-and-seventy-five troops of a Colorado cavalry in a surprise attack, despite ongoing peace negotiations in Denver promising protection for the tribes. The atrocities committed by hundreds of volunteer members of the attacking militia led by Colonel Chivington were beyond imagination or description and included scalping, mutilations, and far worse. When the circumstances became known after Colonel Chivington bragged of his conquests and displayed gruesome anatomical souvenirs as proof, military investigations revealed the truth of the heinous betrayal and mass murder. Multiple witnesses corroborated the horrors they saw and the military tribunals determined that Colonel Chivington had gone rogue and dishonored the nation. Chivington resigned to evade punishment. This was of little comfort to those in the Indian Nation who heard the story. Once again, the tribes had been deceived and forsaken by the white settlers and their government.

Chapter 5

Cataclysmic Changes

The Civil War had taken a catastrophic toll on the previously booming frontier towns. In December of 1862, Van Buren fell to the victorious Union troops who wasted no time in the senseless destruction of printing presses, steamboats and ferry boats, court records, and the cotton factory. The following year, Union troops secured Fort Smith. Though fierce rampages and battles continued for two more years, leaving much of the state dysfunctional and in ruins, the Confederate forces were unable to rout the Union forces. In 1865, Arkansas officially surrendered and was readmitted back into the union three years later.

In January of 1863, the Emancipation Proclamation freed the slaves that were in the ten rebelling Confederate states; however, the war raged on for two more years. Not until the 13th amendment was passed in 1865 were all slaves and indentured servants freed. Trade and commerce halted as savage fighting in the lawless Indian Territories continued. In 1863, the federal troops regained control of the lands and rebuilt Fort Gibson in the Territories. The garrison had originally been established in 1824 to further policies of expansionism and the Indian Removals. Fort

Gibson offered relative protection for escaped slaves and for the Native American tribes. When the Civil War broke out, the federal military resumed control and the community flourished as more people fled to seek safety near the fort. In the summer of that year, in the Muscogee District of the Creek Nation, Confederate troops were defeated, and slowly the remaining refugees who had holed up in Kansas started the return journey to their devastated land. The continuing slaughter and chaos drove throngs of the displaced onward to the comparative safety of the southern border of the Indian Territories, the banks of the Red River.

By the late spring of 1865, two years after the death of Chief Opothleyahola, news of the surrender of the Confederate government had spread throughout the Indian Territories. In April of the same year, President Lincoln was assassinated. The War Between the States had raged for four long years. A formal declaration of the end was declared in 1866 by President Johnson. Finally, the bloody, savage war that had taken the lives of over six hundred and twenty thousand soldiers and an estimated two hundred thousand civilians ended. More than sixty-five percent of those who died during the War Between the States died from disease and lack of medicines. The most common surgical operations performed on the battle field were amputations, leaving the thousands who survived the unanesthetized and unsanitary removal of a limb or an eye, maimed for life.

Negotiating new treaties with the victorious federal government brought further betrayals for the Indian Nation. With punishing severity, the federal government forced the decimated tribes to cede half of the land previously assigned to them to alien tribes from other states who were to be relocated to the Indian Territories. In no position to fight, the Five Civilized Tribes lost the western half of the Indian Nation, which later became known as the Oklahoma Territories. Other conditions set by the federal government ultimately succeeded in stripping any remaining power from the leaders of the Indian nations. Two railroad right-of-ways through the territory were granted and the tribes in a futile attempt to negotiate property rights formed an inter-tribal council with a representative from each tribe. Identified as Freedmen, all slaves of Native Americans were freed and granted tribal citizenship.

The massive business endeavors, including a coast-to-coast railroad network that would ultimately transform the nation, were being negotiated in the late eighteen fifties by competing interests and wealthy businessmen had been delayed and resumed with explosive speed and energy. The Homestead Act, passed a few years earlier, paved the way for hundreds of thousands of people to become land owners, with many pioneers heading for Iowa, Nebraska, and Kansas.

Miraculously, the nation had not been severed and, with the war finally over, rebuilding and reenergizing the economy was embraced exuberantly by the citizens. The streets of Van Buren and other frontier towns swirled with frenzied business deals as shops, lumberyards, liveries, banks, and hardware businesses tried to cope with great streams of people headed further west. Creeks, Cherokees, Seminoles, and their freed slaves, newly arrived European immigrants, trappers, buffalo hunters, wagon builders, saloon keepers, whiskey makers, peddlers, and sly shysters of all sorts filled the streets, each pursuing his trade while searching for a way to make or save another silver dollar. The seemingly boundless frontier mesmerized residents and transients with its promise of endless opportunities and boundless wealth for all.

Reconstruction, after the great and devastating war between the northern and southern states, focused on the most important mission: integration and reunification of the nation, the *United* States. Opportunities supported by the federal government after reconstruction granted education for the newly freed slaves and pathways to private ownership of land or business. As people set about rebuilding lives and homesteads, neighbors helped neighbors in the booming settlement of Van Buren. Van Buren, a frontier and port city on the Arkansas River, had long been a thriving and heavily trafficked city. Steamboats delivered cargo from New Orleans and Ohio, while prospectors, miners, gold dealers, and settlers stocked up on supplies needed for the long and perilous journeys further westward to Santa Fe, New Mexico, or San Francisco, California. Smugglers and outlaws gathered much-needed provisions and stocked up on ammunition, weapons, and alcohol before heading to what later became known as Hell's Fringe, the unmarked gateway to the anarchic and turbulent Indian Territories.

The abolishment of slavery in the newly united nation granted Bass citizenship. Bass Reeves woke to a new day. No longer a fugitive, he was free to live where he pleased. Having adopted many of the characteristics he admired among the tribal communities, Bass adapted enthusiastically to the cataclysmic changes. Calm, fearless, and clever, Bass moved out of the Territories across the river to Van Buren, Arkansas, to start his new life.

After years of witnessing the pain suffered by so many during the war-torn years and having had to rely on his ingenuity to survive the numerous trials that faced him, Bass yearned for a time of relative stability and security. A family, a home, and the prospect of future prosperity were now certainly possible. The wonder of living a lawful, free life filled Bass with power and strength. As everyone in the diverse community sought to build new lives and embraced the end of the bitter war, racial tensions and political ideologies were overshadowed by expectant excitement for the future and relief that the war that had threatened to permanently divide the union was over.

Although vengeance and savagery did surface sporadically, it was a time to rejoice and rebuild for the majority of people. Although everyone had suffered great losses, there seemed to be an unspoken consensus to move forward with optimism and leave the past buried in the past. On the frontier, only the closest of friends or neighbors shared personal tragedies of the war times, so eager was the population to embrace peace and opportunity. There would be time enough in the future to weigh the cost of the war and remember the heavy losses. Young, unemployed Confederate and Union soldiers, with no war to fight, sought adventure and prosperity in the unsettled territories further west. Thousands sought land to homestead.

Preceded by his reputation as a fierce and loyal defender of the weak, Bass Reeves was welcomed to the town where he had lived until the age of eight before his master moved to Texas. The historic significance of the times was not lost on Bass as he joined the throngs of others eager to start a business, find a home or a farm, and explore all the opportunities that living in peace offered.

Chapter 6

Brave New Times

Bass searched the surrounding area of Van Buren for a spot to call his own. He sought fertile land with a source of water, suited for raising both crops and cattle. Within a few weeks, Bass purchased on credit a small spread with groves of wooded areas in gently rolling terrain, a sizable pond, and flat rich land on the west side of the property. When the local dowser assured Bass that there was an abundant source of water on the spot where Bass imagined his future house, any doubts Bass had about the property evaporated. Accompanied by his old friend, Jackson Longarm, who offered to help Bass with the necessary paperwork, Bass went to the bank.

Bass met Jackson Longarm before the War Between the States when he lived with the Creek community. Nearly four decades earlier, Jennie's grandmother, pregnant with the child of her master, had escaped from Alabama with her older brother into the Indian Nations and found refuge among the Creeks. Her daughter, Susanna Little Owl, married Jackson Longarm, son of a local trapper and hunter. It was Jackson who made it possible for Bass to meet Chief Opothleyahola when Bass had first sought safe haven in the Creek lands. Jackson and his wife, Susanna, became fast friends with Bass who helped Jackson take care of his horses and small field of corn. Jackson and Bass often fished and hunted together while Susanna managed the home front and took care of their young daughter, Jennie. Five years later when Confederate soldiers tried to establish a foothold in the Territories and conscript tribal members to fight the Union forces, Jackson and Bass made plans to ride with Opothleyahola who had been promised safety in Kansas. Susanna tearfully remained behind to take care of and protect their young daughter and Susanna's aging parents. When Jackson returned home weeks later, only Susanna and his daughter greeted him. Her parents and their neighbors had succumbed to the mysterious coughing illness that plagued many of the elderly. Jackson, Susannah, and their child, Jennie, determined to survive the cruel winter and the devastating war, stayed close to home and prepared for the worst. In the horrific ongoing chaos of the times, four springs later, Jackson lost Susanna in a savage attack by unknown murderers who had knifed the doomed woman when she unexpectedly interrupted three thieves leading two of their horses out of their corral. Jackson was inconsolable and Bass convinced Jackson and his seventeen-year-old daughter to move across the river to Arkansas about the same time that Bass did. The savagery and hardships of the past five years had taken their toll on everyone and Jackson was not alone in his search for a safer and more prosperous life for his daughter, Jennie, who was now almost an adult.

With the help of friends, Jackson and his daughter opened a small but flourishing supply store selling sugar, coffee, flour, nails, hammers, axes, and saddles. In the summer and fall, Jennie's garden produced a bounty of vegetables which she sold at the store to both residents and travelers passing through. Enterprising and industrious, Jennie added homemade bread and fruit pies to her corner of the shop. With an eye to the future, Jennie watched her hidden stash of cash grow. A blue and white crockery pot bursting with native wild grasses and dried flowers on a kitchen shelf innocently hid the coins and bills secreted inside.

Jennie was as strikingly lovely as Bass was handsome. When her dad and Bass visited together, Jenny busied herself with small tasks. Six-foot-two, slim, and strong, Bass wore a tall black hat and dressed more fashionably than most in that rough time. His easy, wide smile, bushy mustache, and intelligent eyes enhanced his impressive appearance. Almost approaching his third decade, and an eligible bachelor of some fame, Bass continued to attract the attention of both widowed and unmarried women.

On the day that the property sale cleared, Bass celebrated by inviting his friend Jackson Longarm and his alluring daughter, Jennie, to go to the local target competition and community fair on the river bank the following weekend. When Jenny unexpectedly sensed his eyes anchoring on her, she smiled shyly. A fleet flickering glance at him betrayed her confused feelings. Though several younger and admiring would-be suitors attempted to impress Jennie and had also invited her to accompany them to the fair, she remained aloof and disinterested. Aware of his daughter's lengthier-than-usual grooming preparations and her new fondness for staring into the oval mirror in their entryway, Jackson chuckled quietly as he realized how pleased his wife would have been to witness Jennie's transformation into a lovely and gracious young woman. Clearly, Jennie was eagerly anticipating the day of festivities on the river bank the following Saturday.

On that Saturday, Jennie selected a flattering dress and shawl to wear and packed up two of her pecan pies in a basket in preparation for the outing. Jennie felt unusually anxious as she waited with great anticipation for Bass's arrival. She felt much like she had at age thirteen when she had a crush on Isaac, the son of another one of her father's friends. Shyness did not come naturally to Jennie and, unused to the curious feeling, she often wished she had a mother or a sister to share a secret with. *Impossible to discuss this strange feeling with Dad*, she decided.

Shortly before noon, Jennie peered out the open window to watch for Bass's arrival. His erect posture accenting his height as he galloped into their spread caused an unseemly flutter and sudden nervousness as she placed the freshly baked pies in a large wicker basket. Bass greeted her politely and, after a short chat with her father, the trio headed for the path that meandered from the edge of town toward the river bank.

A large crowd had already gathered and the colorful scene reflected the diversity that so characterized the frontier. The linguistic cornucopia that resulted from the flow of multiple and diverse accents and regional dialects was accompanied by expansive and fanciful gestures meant to clarify misunderstandings or emphasize the significance of the thrilling stories that were shared among the fair goers. Like multiple threads, stories about past dangers and tragic losses twisted together with dreams about future opportunities, prosperity, and peace, creating a tapestry textured with complexity and color. A palpable excitement pulsed through all activities.

Fringing the central clearing, several enterprising families had set up canvas awnings under which women were busily selling slices of apple strudel and berry pies as they served up sweet lemonade and cool spring water to thirsty customers. Three Hungarian sisters, well known in the community for their tasty rugelach and apricot marmalade, had already sold out by noon.

Next to a grove of nearby cottonwoods with their leaves rattling lightly and melodically in the breeze, men tended fires beneath huge bellied cast iron cauldrons simmering with beef or chicken stews. Children were recruited to turn the spit for the rabbits slowly grilling nearby. Further off, two suckling pigs roasted in a shallow pit covered with cornstalk leaves and wet burlap bags.

Many had traveled far and camped at the site the night before. A crude sign featuring a roasting pig and a strutting turkey pointed towards the stand of cottonwoods. A couple of itinerant tinkers and peddlers set up their eclectic array of wares on colorful, broadly striped blankets. Small hand tools, packets of needles, playing cards, glass vials of unknown potions and healing herbs, dress patterns, calico and lace, song books, pocket combs, and hand mirrors attracted a constant stream of eager customers. Old Red Dog, a longtime friend of Bass and Jackson from the old days, hung cooking utensils from a makeshift rack of dead branches. The pleasant clinking of the utensils, as they swayed gently on the branches, stirred Bass with an unexpected longing for comfort and stability in his life. Slowly and thoughtfully, Bass turned from Red Dog and glanced at Jennie who was engaged in a lively exchange punctuated by laughter and whispers with two friends. A strange sensation rippled through him. Bass felt oddly timid and wondered what secret topic they discussed that caused them to laugh and whisper. When Jennie suddenly looked up, Bass flushed, politely touched his hat brim, and walked briskly away. Bass, unfamiliar with feeling self-conscious, was suddenly in a hurry to join a small audience watching two men wrestle on a nearby grassy patch. Bass distracted himself from his unsettling feelings by volunteering to referee the impromptu matches.

Groups of tribal men wearing narrow-brimmed tall black hats and colorful vests ornamented with beads or feathers mingled with settlers and frontier farmers. Young Cherokee men were easily identified by their arresting hair styles, a kind of fringe on top of their otherwise hairless heads. Some attached feathers to one long lock of hair trailing down the nape of their necks. Young women wore their long shiny hair loose, draped over their shoulders, coiled in buns, or braided with feathers and ribbons. Handsomely beaded headbands and deerskin moccasins were available for trade or purchase. Pioneer women and tribal women worked side by side, gathering dried wood for campfires and spreading out blankets under scattered trees. The diversity of clothing among the women included the currently popular gingham dresses while some women decked themselves out in layered skirts or shorter deerskin shifts. Bobbing and nodding heads sported bonnets, straw hats, shawls, or scarves of every hue. In the shade of a wild crabapple tree, an unfamiliar group of women danced with small bells tied to their ornately beaded moccasins. Smoke from various cooking fires curled through the brisk autumn air and the smell of roasting apples, onions, and meat stimulated the appetites of all.

The collective euphoria that permeated through the crowds inspired fantastical tale-telling. Although it was acceptable to ask where a family or individual came from, it was an unspoken understanding that only the boorish would question why they had left their home states or countries. The answers could only have been one of a few and everyone recognized the common bond they shared. Whether the reason had to do with famine or politics in their home country, abuse, abandonment, lack of opportunity, poverty, political threat, or the past brutal civil war, it was understood that everybody was prepared to risk all for a chance to grab the brass ring on the carousel of life. Enthusiastic and energetic, the young were eager to follow their dreams, and the older men and women were grateful for another chance to shape their future. For many, a miss could be no worse than what they had left. For others, powerful curiosity and the thrill of exploring the unknown were enough reasons to propel those seekers further westward.

Of great interest to many at the fair were the stories told by the cowboys and drifters who found a rapt audience. They traded stories about rough and burly trail bosses, river crossings, and harrowing cattle stampedes on the highly trafficked Chisholm Trail that crossed through the Comanche and Kiowa lands and onwards through the "Unassigned Lands" as the cattlemen wound their way from Texas to the stockyards in Abilene or Wichita, Kansas. Positions and specific tasks of the men on the trail were assigned on the basis of experience, with newbies given the unpleasant chore of drag riders who followed the herd, keeping stragglers and slow movers on the trail. The most talented of cowboys was employed in the enviable position of the point man leading the herd. Older, experienced men served as the wranglers who took care of the horses, or, in the most esteemed position, as the trail boss.

The young cowboys, most between the ages of fourteen and eighteen, were adventurers and sprang from every walk of life. The trail bosses welcomed the arrival of ever more greenhorns willing to join the great drives. The now-unemployed soldiers from the Union and the

Confederacy, freed slaves, Native Americans, newly-arrived immigrants, orphans, and young boys running away from home made up the diverse and motley population.

There were few conflicts between the cowmen and cow boys while on the trail. With the average drive taking four months, covering about ten miles a day, the need for cooperation and mutual help demanded amity and unity in dealing with the daily dangers the sixty or seventy men faced in common. The great cattle trails crossed through the Indian lands and both the cattle industry and the indigenous people benefitted from the agreement. In addition to the famed cattle trail, the Chisholm Trail, three other major trails crossed through the Unassigned Lands' middle point of the Indian Nation.

Hostile Comanche or Kiowa warriors expected payment for passing through their lands and the demands were always met. Angry young warriors could easily rile the cattle with piercing shrieks or noise makers to cause a dangerous and uncontrollable mass panic. Two drovers, both wearing leather chaps, bragged about successfully moving three thousand head of Longhorn cattle across the muddy Cimarron River just east of the Cheyenne Arapaho reservation. Changes in weather, especially at night, were a common cause of stampedes and the drovers and trail bosses were always on high alert for a flash of lightning or a sudden clap of thunder that would announce an incoming storm. Controlling a large frightened bellowing herd of two and a half thousand or three thousand head of longhorn cattle was no easy feat, and the experienced drovers under the direction of the trail boss worked together to bring the herd into an ever-tightening circle. To entertain themselves and keep the herd soothed, the drovers sang as they circled around the cattle. Whether the songs they sang were in Spanish, English, or any other language, the trail lullabies, ballads, gospel songs, and the old miners' ditties calmed both beast and man.

Stories of catastrophes, deaths, and dangerous encounters with outlaw gangs on the long cattle drives of one thousand miles from Texas to Kansas, or further north to Chicago, exhilarated the audience of mostly young, strong men who longed for the countless and heroic adventures that awaited them should they travel further west.

When no women were present to listen to the wild tales of the cowboys, a few of the older men would pull the spell bound innocents aside. With sly winks and gap-toothed grins, they confided to the boys that a few nights of relaxation in the lawless cow-town of Abilene, which at any time boasted at least ten brothels, would guarantee them a unique education they would be taxed to find in their home towns. They praised the special humor and kindness of a Miss Rita Mae and her affectionate friends. Miss Rita Mae's friends from southern and northern states, the stateless territories, and from south of the border were as diverse as the cattle men and cowboys. Rita Mae was a popular and wise woman, a woman who could erase the aches and saddle sores of the trail men, a woman who understood the trials of riding the trail and welcomed all of the weary transients who rested in Abilene after the long and challenging trail journey.

When the lengthy cattle drive came to an end or a rest in Abilene, the two to three thousand cattle would be corralled off in the stockade just outside of town. On the trail for more than four months, the men were eager for a shave and haircut, a hot bath, a soft mattress, good meals, and ready to welcome whatever the town could offer. As the customers-to-be poured into town, Miss Rita Mae would make sure any who wanted could have their first beer or shot of fire water, on her tab, gratis. It was rumored that Miss Mae was a great markswoman and packed two pistols in the rare cases it was necessary to protect any of her employees from piggish behavior or crude insults. That a few nights of rip-roaring entertainment, gambling, and whiskey, or becoming more closely acquainted with Miss Rita Mae and her agreeable friends could easily cost an entire paycheck, was not encouraging information and best not mentioned. Nor did the story tellers reveal intimate particulars about the incurable and painful illness that afflicted many of the cowboys weeks after wild reveling in the bordellos after pay day. Personal details were only shared on the trail, if at all.

Young men listened to the tales with great attention and excitement, giving no thought to the hardships such a rough lifestyle promised. Many of the cowboys were skilled story tellers and knew how to rouse the admiring crowd with a deft weaving of facts that emphasized the conquests and successes of their escapades. They omitted tales about the deaths of comrades, dreadful accidents, and too frequent river drownings. They were silent also about the dog days of the sultry summer with its scorching heat, the unending clouds of dust stirred up by the cattle, the grimy grit that coated the cowboys head to toe, the monotonous meals, and the constant fear of hostile attack or stampedes. For some men, the pleasurable respite offered in the stockyard towns was an incentive to endure the hardships on the trail.

While many embraced the challenges of the long, rough drives, some of the cowboys discovered that the anticipated days of glory were more absent than present. For some of the greenhorn cowboys, one cattle drive was enough to satisfy their youthful curiosity. Images of tall leafy trees, grassy meadows, towering mountains, and rushing rivers further west beckoned and they hastened to explore opportunities that were less dangerous and physically demanding than the life of a cowboy on the trail.

Of particular interest to the listeners was the town of Abilene, and the cowboys were eager to answer all questions. Until 1871, Abilene had no law officer, and all disputes, whether born of drink, greed, or love, were resolved by gun. It was a rare quarrel between the men that could be settled by a mere fist fight. In 1871, when Wild Bill Hickok was tasked with the dangerous job of marshaling the unbridled and turbulent town, violent activities decreased as evident by greatly reduced homicide statistics. Each new parade of cow hands and cattle brought unexpected trouble, and Wild Bill, often enjoying a peaceful afternoon with Miss Rita Mae and her friends at the Alamo Saloon only a block north of Main Street, would fold his cards, pull on his vest and, with a quick glance in the gilded mirror over the bar counter, he would check the silver star on his lapel, adjust his hat, and then holster up before striding out down the street to boldly face the grievance of the day. Wild Bill was already becoming a legend and several townspeople confirmed the story tellers' tales, attesting to Wild Bill's liberalness and tolerance of the transients and cow hands that streamed endlessly through the town of Abilene.

Bass and Jennie, both friendly and communicative, enjoyed the stories they heard and the colorful characters that peopled the scene. One old-timer, heavily bearded, and, despite the balmy autumn weather, warmly wrapped in a homemade patchwork vest of multicolored furs and a peculiarly shaped hat made of red fox fur, rested against a knobby old cedar tree next to a slowly trickling creek. A brightly beaded knife sheath hung from his waist. When he unloaded two large stacks of beaver and otter pelts and draped the soft skins over a plaited leather cord attached to two stakes, he found himself immediately circled by a loquacious group of prospective buyers who murmured to themselves as they fondled and caressed the soft furs. Long inured to the idle chatter of fellow men, the old trapper was at first reticent to speak and only pointed to the skins, counting numbers by holding up the crooked fingers of his gnarled hand. Bass and Jenny wandered over and sat on the ground next to him. Unable to sustain his obdurate manner in the face of Bass's hearty questioning and Jenny's warm smile, the old man settled against the tree trunk and delivered a lengthy assessment of the state of the new union as he saw it.

With slow and deliberate enunciation, he mourned the momentous changes sweeping through the country. Unlike most of the younger frontiersmen, who were intoxicated with glorious visions of what the future promised, the aging trapper felt an overwhelming sadness and anger at the inevitable losses that development and progress brought to his world. Railroad tracks were insidiously snaking through the frontier, dividing the ancient migration routes of the vast buffalo herds. Already in the late 1860s, the herds that used to stretch as far as the eye could see were visibly diminishing. With the beaver population depleted by over hunting and trapping, more traders shifted their interests to the buffalo. He suspected that the indiscriminate killings, mostly done in the winter, when the hides were thick and furry, were beginning to take a toll on the tribal communities who depended on the mighty beasts for food and clothing.

The old man could not have imagined the brutal slaughtering of the immense herds that would tremendously escalate the following year with the completion of the Pacific Transcontinental Railroad in 1869. Hundreds of crazed men would travel from the East and use the trains as shooting platforms. As the trains kept pace with the vast herds, the hunters fired wildly in a senseless competition to slay as many buffalos as possible. Nothing of the carcasses was salvaged by the bloodthirsty sportsmen and the bodies were left to rot in the sun. One hunter boasted that he had killed a total of six thousand buffaloes on multiple hunting expeditions. Recently, a stampeding herd of several hundred bison had derailed a train as the panicked beasts charged across the tracks. More than twenty men had been crushed to death under the pounding hooves, a just death for the cruel sportsmen, the old man felt. The completion of the Trans-Continental Railroad, a momentous and historic feat, would change the nation forever, the old man lamented. With the completion of each rail line section, saloons, brothels, and gaming halls sprang up overnight, catering to the vices of unsavory drifters and cowboys hungry for women, alcohol, and games of chance. Gambling disagreements that quickly escalated into fist fights or shootouts in front of a tavern or brothel encouraged further anarchy and mayhem, the trapper cursed. The blasting whistles and clanking engines spewing black smoke into the crystal-pure air were deplored by the old trapper.

Gone were the days when the trapper could walk weeks without seeing any other man, or even months, as had his father before him. Friends with tribal chiefs, with whom he had traded over the past forty years, the old man grieved at their loss of independence and ancestral ways. He cursed the evil war between the northern and the southern states that had brought unbidden misery, betrayal, and death to the native communities.

When asked by a bystander listening in to the conversation about his opinion on the causes of the war, a grimace flickered across his face and he turned away and stared at the creek. That vicious war had nothing to do with him. The bystander, concluding that the old man was hard of hearing, tipped his hat and wandered off to find a livelier person to converse with. The old man raked his hand across the ground in front of him and slowly tossed a few small pebbles, one by one, into the creek. He and Bass gazed at the steady widening of the circles of ripples. Each lost in their own thoughts but aware of an unspoken understanding between the two of them, Bass tossed another pebble into the creek. It was a few moments before the old trapper resumed conversation.

The old man was equally distraught about a new type of fencing that was sure to be the deathblow to the open range and the cattle drives. The newly popular "Devil's Rope" made of knotted and pointy wires with needle-like barbs caused great injuries and infections for the cattle. Now under attack by the evil spikey wire fences, the days of free-roaming by both cattle and cowboys were soon coming to an ignoble end and would be remembered only in the words of songs and the dimming memories of old men. He could not imagine the vast and beautiful prairies and grassland corralled in by miles of the barbed fencing. The elderly dreamer compared the prairie to a magnificent living creature soon to be cruelly reined in and harnessed with the torturous Devil's Rope.

The unctuous voice of deceit concealing a hand of greed had brought nothing but poverty, illness, and infinite sorrow to his friends. The tribes would never recover from these betrayals, predicted the old timer, and, like their beloved buffaloes, they would fade back to the spirit world. Their voices would echo across the land in the howls of wolves and coyotes, the call of owls, and the moaning winds of the distant prairies. With a gesture of futility, the old man waved his hand towards a small group of children playing hide-and-seek and two older boys crouched on the ground shooting marbles into a ring sketched out in the hard earth. Those children would never know his world, the old man commented. Like the thundering Niagara River plunging over Horseshoe Falls, the future onslaught was powerful and unstoppable. His pale eyes, clouded by cataracts, stared past Bass and Jennie, across the river to the as-yet stateless land. He shrugged in defeat. His arthritic hand trailed slowly and fondly over the lined-up pelts. Jennie bought several small pieces to shape and use as linings in shoes before they left. The old man, with his sad reminisces and prophetic visions, raised his hand to his curiously shaped fur hat when Bass and Jennie thanked him for his company and waved goodbye. A few years later, Jennie and Bass would revisit the conversation they had that autumn afternoon and remark on the prescience of the old trapper, whose bleak vision of the future had indeed unfolded.

An elderly fiddler with his twin grandsons decked out in matching collarless shirts and bandannas, attracted a small crowd who stamped appreciatively while clapping to the beat of the increasingly frenzied music. A medley of improvised instruments being played nearby—the rhythmic and hypnotic strumming of a washboard, rapid clinking of spoons, and makeshift drums from empty jugs—added to the musical entertainment. Spread out on woven blankets or quilts, adults played checkers. The children gazed at the sky and, in hushed tones, identified familiar forms they recognized in the slowly shifting clouds as they morphed from one illusive creature to another.

Horses, mules, and ponies were corralled nearby in a fenced-off area. Boys assigned to watch them hooted as they chased each other, absorbed in their wild gambols, paying little heed to the responsibility charged to them. Three or four shifty characters, hats pulled low over their foreheads and engrossed in an animated discussion, slyly eyed the horses as a blindfolded boy chased the others in the age-old game of Blind Man's Bluff.

Just across the river lay the lawless land of the Indian Territories. The children stared across the dark and muddy waters of the Arkansas River, whispering to each other the stories that they had overheard frightened parents share about the dangerous desperadoes, escaped criminals, and horse thieves who hid there. Holding his father's coveted collapsible telescope to his eye, young Gustaf Knut and his twin sister, Hanna, passed the wondrous spyglass back and forth, imagining they could see a gang of murderous rebels on a small hill just north of the scrubby thicket of blackjack trees that fringed the western bank of the river. Gustaf handed the slick brass tube to Bass who marveled at the curved lenses that could so easily make the unseen seen. *A pocket telescope would be useful*, Bass mused.

The celebratory atmosphere encouraged friendly mingling and shared camaraderie among most, though a few disgruntled men with permanent scowls carved in their hardened faces kept to themselves, passing a ceramic flask around their circle. When Bass noticed several people casting a wary eye at the group camped near the make shift stockade, he walked over, humming softly to himself, and introduced himself to the first man who leaped up as he approached. As if attacked by a swarm of hornets, the others scrambled up quickly. Although no one could hear what Bass said to the group, it was clear that his smiling warning had been effective. Within minutes, the ruffians saddled up their horses and tore off. The random shots they fired as they jabbed spurs into hide, startled protective parents who had been unaware of the brief confrontation.

Bass's ability as a superb gunman, coupled with his ingenuity in the face of deception, was a highly desirable skill in the generally lawless times that followed. In fact, Bass was often relied on to strike fear when needed, and Bass was happy to oblige his neighbors when called upon. His excellent marksmanship excluded him from entering local target competitions, but his presence at such events was gladly received as he was a spirited supporter and always a fair judge of close calls. After the official competition ended and the winner was announced, Bass would accept challenges from the winners in an unofficial, but impressive display of his skills. Having no rivals in wrestling, Bass was often persuaded to serve as a judge for the matches that often followed a target shooting tournament. His deep voice bellowing out judgment calls identifying the victor was never challenged by the enthusiastic knot of men and boys who followed every turn and twist of each wrestler.

Jenny was much taken by the bravado and intelligence of Bass. She found pleasure every evening in recording in her journal the sweet temptations that marked the eight-week courtship with Bass Reeves. His friendship with her father dated from the times that preceded that fierce War Between the States, and she delighted in the bond they shared. Though she did not know the secrets her father and Bass Reeves shared, she trusted their measurement of the transforming events of the time and their optimistic view of the future. Jenny embraced the rising tidal wave of social change that promised to supplant the existing boundaries between men and women, master and slave, state and territory, the old government, and all those who dreamed of beginning new lives in the rapidly expanding nation.

Intuition persuaded her to be patient as she waited to gain Bass's full confidence and attention. Bass now dropped by nearly every evening, ostensibly to visit with her father. More often than not, he showed up in the late afternoon and Jenny made sure to have pies or desserts on hand or even a light supper in case Bass would linger longer at the house. Now and then, Bass would suggest that the three of them go for a short walk to admire the spectacular glowing sunsets near the pond. Jackson accompanied them the first couple of times but deferred for future walks. His excuses were weak but neither Bass nor Jennie insisted too much.

When Bass invited Jennie to walk with him on an early evening stroll a few weeks later, explaining he had something special to show her, she felt both expectant and intuitively certain of a shared future. For some reason, Bass was not as talkative as usual, and Jennie did not interrupt the curious, but comfortable, silence. They walked slowly toward the pond on the property, their favored site. The Mexican feather grass, ringing the western side of the pond, sparkled in the fading sunlight. Caressed by a soft breeze, the long silky white plumes swayed gently in unison, like the long feathers of an exotic white-tailed rooster Jennie had seen at the neighbor's farm. Jennie never forgot the beauty of the moment, nor the utter peace she felt that evening. As was Bass's custom, he threw two pebbles from the bank to the center of the still water. This time though, Bass reached for her hand and held it firmly as they silently watched the gentle waves of the ripples approach the edge. She thought she heard him murmur something quietly about *a stone thrown* before he cupped her small shoulders in his large hands and turned her to face him. Bass was more than a foot taller than Jennie and, when he leaned over and tucked a spiral of hair behind her ear, she knew he would whisper the words she had so patiently waited to hear. She did not hesitate to accept Bass's proposal that memorable evening.

Returning to the cabin, Jackson greeted them and smiled broadly when Bass, as custom directed, asked him for Jennie's hand. The three made simple plans for a wedding to be held a few weeks later, time enough to get word out to invited guests. Their marriage, celebrated by neighbors and friends, included old companions and relatives from the Indian Territory who crossed the river and joined in the festivities. Minewa and Tuska-homa surprised the couple with generous gifts, that included a large tanned buffalo hide to be used as a rug and a fine array of hand-woven baskets. After the celebration, Bass and Jennie noticed that an elaborately beaded and painted cradleboard had been placed under the willow tree near the house by anonymous well-wishers who hoped the new couple would enjoy a fruitful and happy union.

It was truly the start of a new life for everyone in the community. Neighbors helped neighbors build houses and corrals. The communal effort to rebuild lives encouraged optimism among all and helped vanquish the bitter and dark memories of the terrible war they had managed to survive. It was time to embrace the future. Bass and Jennie's simple two-story frame house became a home in no time. A garden of corn and tomatoes, peppers, carrots, and potatoes supplied their household with year-round vegetables. Bass managed an ever-growing small herd of cattle and attended to his fine horses. Magic, very much older and slower, had served Bass well and was treated to a comfortable and well-fed retirement in the small pasture near the pond. Bass, an ardent dog lover, and his two hunting dogs, Ajax and Sadie, trotted with Bass as he carried out the daily chores or went hunting in the nearby woods.

Hard work and Bass's expertise as a stockman, coupled with his numerous connections and popularity within the vigorously flourishing community, rewarded the young family with economic prosperity. Bass and Jennie were eager to have a family and their first three children were born in quick succession, with seven more babies to follow during the next decade. Jennie busied herself with child care, gardening, cooking, and sewing, all of which she did with enthusiasm and affection. Her patience, humor, and good nature were a comfort to Bass who loved to be home with his family. Spending time with his children and Jennie was a welcome respite from the perilous life he led on many volunteer missions accompanying marshals in the unending effort by Judge Parker to bring fugitives hiding out across the river to his court. Jennie was popular in the community and her generosity was appreciated by the neighbors and towns folk. Fortunate was the family who received one of Jennie's quilts as a gift to welcome a new born child or a homemade pie to celebrate a birthday. Jennie's kindness and willingness to help others were characteristics that never failed to move Bass. He too was generous, always offering to help a neighbor or friend in need. It was not unusual for him to hand out silver dollars he earned from his multiple enterprises to a family or individual who had suffered hard luck.

Chapter 7

Frontier Thrills and Challenges for Bass

As the Reeves family grew larger, roomy additions were added to the wood frame house. A large wrap-around porch, trellised on three sides with lilac and trumpet vines, offered a shady retreat for the family and the numerous, diverse guests who came to visit on hot summer nights to share news, play a hand of whist, or a game of dominoes, and share a plentiful meal.

The hospitality of Bass and Jennie excluded no one and a steady flow of welcomed visitors trailed through their home. Good friends of Bass included several Freedmen, the term used to describe those slaves of both the Native Americans and the white southerners who had been given their freedom in the 1860s by the federal government. Many of the Freedmen worked with the Indian Lighthorse Police officers, who, in turn, worked for the Indian Agencies of the federal government. In 1876, the individual tribal agencies merged and were tasked with representing the interests of the Five Civilized Tribes, while, at the same time, doing all possible to further assimilation. Serving mostly in the Indian Territories, the Lighthorse Police had the authority to arrest any tribal member accused of a crime and they assisted the federal Indian Agents. They also guarded stagecoaches carrying cash and ambushed horse and cattle thieves hiding in the canyons and hills of the Sans Bois Mountains. The Lighthorse Police captain and his troop of riders roamed through all tribal lands, offering protection to victims of outlaws, turning over fugitives and felons to the US marshals, and, at times, meting out justice themselves. One of the most important and difficult tasks of the Indian police was to make sure the federal laws prohibiting the sale and manufacture of alcohol were enforced. All attempts to control the flow of liquor in the Territories brought in by smugglers, who eagerly supplied tribal members and fugitives with illegal beer and whiskey, seemed doomed to failure.

The continually increasing number of illegal settlers and farmers boldly trying to settle into the Indian lands, despite treaties and laws protecting the Indian Nation, was alarming. Whether the federal government would continue to honor agreements and protect the tribes was a frequently discussed and controversial topic that contributed to growing divisiveness. The diverse and dehumanized Indian population of the Five Civilized Tribes, so-called because of their initial willingness to assimilate with the prevailing culture, had been relocated to the vast 'reservation'. They tried to sustain a living, but the stateless land reserved for the tribes tempted many unscrupulous squatters, and it was the perilous duty of these Lighthorse Mounted Police to remove them.

Of interest to all in the frontier towns were the stories about pioneer families traveling together in long strings of wagon trains. Beyond the limits of civilization and easy comfort, the families, like a community, worked and lived together on the trail, helping each other. Covering twelve miles in one day was considered a good pace but often less was covered in a day. The lengthy and arduous trek of several months necessitated tending to the sick, burying the dead, birthing new babies, sharing food, and protecting each other. As they faced the challenges of crossing mountains, fording rivers, violent weather, damaged wagons, and hostile tribes, friendship and mutual support among the settlers were essential for survival and completion of the journey. Only a few foolhardy families traveled the trail alone.

The horrific tale of the recently emigrated German family traveling west to Santa Fe from Missouri was well known and often retold. It was a tale of warning and confirmed the undeniable truth that traveling solo across the vast prairies or the Rocky Mountains was a folly that only the naïve or reckless would undertake. The Gunderson family of four was attacked, brutally scalped, and slaughtered by barbarous killers, renegades who banded together after being exiled from the rivaling Comanche and Apache tribes on the western edge of the Indian Territories. The cut-throat gang roamed the prairie and kept a sharp eye out for lone families or individuals on the trails that had stubbornly underestimated the perilous journey and traveled without the safety a caravan of multiple wagons under the guidance of a savvy and experienced leader offered. The warriors attacked at dusk, just as the optimistic Gunderson family was wearily, but happily, setting up camp for the night. They savagely murdered the family, leaving their ravaged bodies to the vultures and the elements. Ransacking the wagon, they loaded up weapons, ammunition, blankets, flour, and dry beans. Before setting the small prairie schooner ablaze, they cut loose the Gunderson's three ponies and two oxen, knowing they would easily retrieve the wandering animals later. With lightning speed, the killers raced twenty miles back to the safety of their well-concealed hideout.

A train of eight Conestoga wagons led by Isaac Meriwether warily approached the burnt-out schooner two days later. The charred wagon, missing horses, and mangled bodies heaped in a pile told the gruesome story. The women and children sheltered silently in the wagons while ten men carved out two shallow graves in the hard sunbaked desert and hastily buried the four bodies. Before the caravan moved on, Isaac murmured a short prayer and encouraged the distraught settlers to sing a hymn. One wooden cross with the burial date marked the two graves of the Gunderson family, a chilling warning to those who traveled alone on the challenging Santa Fe Trail that passed through land controlled by the hostile Comanche and Kiowa.

The many stories of dangerous encounters and shifty characters entertained the law-abiding citizens who visited the Reeves household. The most thrilling stories shared among the guests were of stage coach journeys and attacks by notorious outlaws who hid in the Territories. There was much excited talk of the transformational changes in the nation, and while some memories of past heroics or simpler times stirred up nostalgia, other recollections were better left buried in the past.

Tobias Quinn, often a guest at the Reeves home, was a thirty-five-year-old blacksmith. Toby, as his friends called him, had served with the short-lived but famous Pony Express delivery system more than a decade before. Tobias had lost both of his newly immigrated parents to the cholera epidemic in New York City when he was eight years old. With no relatives in the new country, he and his younger sister, Molly, were just two more children to join the two hundred and fifty thousand other homeless or abandoned children put on the Orphan Trains traveling west to St. Louis, Missouri, where they were placed in one of the many orphanages until they were adopted by a family in a farming community. Molly, with her piercing green eyes and amber hair streaked with sun kisses, was shy and clung closely to her brother. Within a few weeks, Molly's placid personality and attractive appearance caught the attention of a middle-aged childless couple from St. Joseph, who adopted her within weeks. To comfort the children who wept at being told of the pending separation, the couple promised to bring Molly to visit Tobias the next month, but Toby never saw his sister again; a fate all too common for orphaned siblings.

Toby's clever and mischievous nature aggravated the sour, easily-rattled mission volunteers and nuns, who, despite their devout commitment to serve a higher calling, lacked both the patience and courage that the secular world demanded. Far easier to punish and lecture the youth than attempt futile communication with such a clever and active boy. The pious sisters prayed for Toby Quinn to share the good fortune of his adopted sister, Molly. The Mother Superior and her flock agreed that a loving and God-fearing family with a firm male hand would be a great blessing to the reckless young boy and, at the same time, heavenly intervention would also free them to address more rewarding responsibilities. Unknown to them, Toby also prayed for release from the restraints of the orphanage and its keepers. He longed for a horse, a dog, the fresh air of the country, a pond to fish in, and a kind family to rescue him.

When Toby turned eleven, both the nuns' and Toby's appeals were finally answered. The feisty rascal was taken in by an older man and his family in need of a strong, spirited boy to help with multiple chores. Toby was delighted to leave the dour nuns and the dark, stuffy institution and welcomed the future. Within a day, his life had changed and he moved to the countryside to his new family's farm. Home maintenance, gardening, cooking meals, and a one-year-old child kept the young wife busy. There was no end to the many chores that Toby worked on under the instruction of her older husband. Toby embraced the change in his life and never complained about the endless tasks. Feeding animals, building fences, hauling water and hay, and tilling the small patch of land filled the day. To his misfortune, this new and stable chapter of his life lasted only a few years before the husband succumbed to the yellow fever epidemic that had claimed more than seven thousand lives in New Orleans in the past year. The mother and the four-year-old toddler sold the small acreage and returned to St. Louis, where her older sister lived. Saddened at the loss of his adopted family, Toby, now almost sixteen years old, struck out alone, determined to find a way to earn his keep. The adversity he had already experienced in his short life gifted Toby with a maturity far beyond his years. So much of Toby's life had been shaped by the need to survive. Philosophical about life and events he could not change, Toby was resilient and knew there was no choice but to accept what the future would bring.

Like a good method actor, Toby adopted the lifestyle and persona of any role he was called upon to play. Practical and clever, the young boy decided to work as an apprentice to the local blacksmith and learn to forge gates, tools, and grills. The endless demand on the frontier for tools of all sorts assured Toby that being a smithy was a respectable trade promising security and prosperity. *It might be boring,* he thought, *but at least I'll earn my own money and learn a trade. Maybe someday, I'll be able to buy a few acres of land, build a home, and have my own business.* Tobias was a talented and fast learner and, within a year, he had easily mastered the necessary skills the blacksmith had taught him. A vague restlessness unexpectedly rippled through him as he shod the third horse of the day and completed work on an iron padlock for the owner of the local pub. At the end of the day, he was sent to deliver the lock and chain to Rufus Miles, the owner.

As he sprinted out of the tavern after a brief chat with Mr. Miles assuring him of the strength and security of the new lock, a partially hand-colored recruitment flyer for the Pony Express nailed on the post near the door of the pub caught his eye. He stopped abruptly to study it. Maybe it was the sketch of a sleek black horse with a rider hunkered down, one hand on his hat, tearing across the open prairies, silhouetted against a blazing orange sunset, that grabbed him.

The next morning, despite the satisfaction he felt from his work training as a smithy, seventeen-year-old Tobias Quinn was unable to resist the call to adventure and, feeling a great surge of excitement, confident that he would be the ideal rider for the much anticipated transcontinental postal delivery system, he eagerly completed the application. He met all the requirements listed in the recruitment ad. Wiry, strong, and skilled with firearms, Toby weighed less than one hundred and twenty-five pounds, and had won several local horse riding competitions. The company notice specified a preference for orphaned young men, who presumably would be free of intervention by protective adults who might try to dissuade their young sons from such a dangerous career.

The pay was a hefty one hundred dollars a month, far more than Toby earned as an assistant to a blacksmith.

Toby was hired immediately and was not disappointed with his new employment. Toby solemnly took the required oath:

"I, Tobias Quinn, do hereby swear, before the Great and Living God, that during my engagement, and while I am an employee of Russell, Majors, and Waddell, I will under no circumstances use profane language, that I will drink no intoxicating liquors, that I will not quarrel or fight with any other member of the firm, and that in every respect I will conduct myself honestly, be faithful to my duties and so direct all my acts to win the confidence of my associates. So help me God!" Toby was then presented with a Bible to be read daily, a gun to be used only in the direst of circumstances, and a leather bag for the mail. The very next day, he was given his first assignment, a short run of forty-five miles.

Even more than a decade later, Toby thrilled his listeners with dramatic stories of the endless adventures, dangers, people, and places he encountered on his many runs before the telegraph put the Pony Express out of business. A well-worn leather mail pouch, the *mochila*, from his last run was a treasured souvenir of his youth. The nearly two thousand mile route from St. Joseph, Missouri, to Sacramento, California, was covered in ten days. Toby regretted not having been to all of the nearly two hundred relay stations, but he told his listeners he had certainly been to half of them. Every fifteen miles or so, he would trade out his tired mount for a fresh mustang, riding a total of eighty to ninety miles a day. The all-time record-breaking run of nearly two thousand miles to deliver President Lincoln's Inaugural Address to the west coast had been accomplished in an astonishing seven and a half days.

He often told the tale of his friend, Pony Bob, who had to fill in for a full second run because the designated rider was too fearful of a band of aggressive Indians sighted earlier on the horizon. Pony Bob covered one hundred and ninety miles exchanging horses every fifteen or twenty miles at the relay stations and wasted no time at any stop, taking less than two minutes to grab his *mochila* and make a speedy switch to a fresh mount. Toby described monstrous roaring tornadoes, blinding dust storms, and treacherous river crossings. Some of the lands he rode through were inhabited by fierce tribes whose warriors sometimes followed him for miles, before fortunately veering off in search of slower and juicier game. The violence of the erratic weather in stark contrast to the breath taking panoramic views of endless mountains and unbroken vistas of the deserts and prairies mesmerized Toby, inspiring the youth to whoop joyfully as he raced on toward the next station. As if his exuberant enthusiasm might stir up hostile activity or even unleash angry weather, the station masters, who kept a sharp lookout out on the horizon for any signs of trouble, felt alarmed by such boisterousness. Tobias only laughed and shouted louder when he noticed their eyes flickering in fear and their grim expressions. Great stamina by the riders was required and, after a hearty breakfast at the station, the jockeys did not eat until the end of their run. Like the other riders, Toby stuffed a breakfast biscuit or two in his vest pocket in case of unexpected trouble on the run. It was always humorous to Bass to imagine the now thirty-two-year-old bearded Toby as a slight young boy racing across the untamed prairies.

There was much talk too at the Reeves family gatherings about the vanishing bison herds and the rail ways that began to slink across the country. Entrepreneurial types made deals with the railroad companies to provide bison meat for the workers building the tracks and provide necessary goods. Bass remembered the sad old man at the fair who had mourned the indiscriminate and contemptible killing of those migratory beasts of the prairies and learned that now, only a few years later, as many as five thousand of the magnificent creatures were slaughtered *every day* by white hunters and wealthy tourists from the East, who traveled to the Midwest solely for the purpose of joining in the sport of extermination. Bison carcasses were no longer left to rot on the open land as they had been before. Now, even the skeletons of the doomed beasts would vanish as bone collectors and children scoured the plains to gather the whitened bones that were used as a filtering component in processing cane sugar. The pulverized bones were needed to supply the booming east coast industries that produced fine chinaware, paints, and fertilizers. Mountains of skulls and bones piled up next to towering heaps of hides. Skilled bison hunters could bring down as many as two hundred and fifty beasts a day. With the going rate of $3.25 for a hide and a tongue, the gruesome occupation could bring in a hefty eight hundred dollars per day; a fortune to industrious hunters.

That the uncontrolled slaughter would soon dry up their gravy train did not give pause. The seemingly endless bounty of the prairie did not encourage circumspection or foresight by those whose livelihoods depended on it. New tanning techniques that softened the tough hides upped the demand by the wealthy for buffalo hides which were fashioned into long stylish coats and lap blankets. Buffalo tongue became popular as a gourmet delicacy in the urban centers of the East, and tens of thousands of bison were slaughtered to extract that one tasty, coveted organ. In 1874, three million pounds of bison bones were loaded onto trains headed north to be used by manufacturers of porcelain wares and fertilizer. Herds that were fifty miles wide and stretched on for a five-day ride had not been uncommon. By 1876, the southern herd of four million bison was totally exterminated, hastening the demise of tribal communities who depended for survival on the herds roaming the open ranges. By the time Congress decided to make a futile move to save the bison, it was too late, and the undulating hills of grazing buffaloes across the Midwestern prairies as far as the eye could see were already a memory of a time now long gone.

One extraordinary tale about a buffalo hunter's gruesome and failed survival attempt was dramatically narrated at the household. A wicked four-day-long blizzard near the Rocky Mountains had surprised a hunter who had just brought down a massive buffalo. The hunter, exhausted but exuberant after the long and successful chase, unpacked his saddle bag to retrieve some dried jerky and hardtack before tackling the bloody job ahead of him. As he admired the size of the grand beast, he gnawed on the jerky and tough hunk of bread. The snow at first fell lightly and softly and the hunter patted the buffalo's head, running his ungloved fingers through the thick curly hair, as he calculated numbers in his head and tried to estimate the market value of the oversized buffalo. As the wind and snow steadily intensified, the hunter looked apprehensively at the sky and pulled his woolen scarf tighter around his neck. Within ten minutes, the softly falling snow blanketed everything in sight. Blinded by the thick snow fall, the hunter could barely make out the dead buffalo or his horse. Only the increasingly whining and whistling winds punctuated the utter silence. The hunter, with a sense of great impending doom, knew the storm was intensifying. He wondered if he would live to describe the eerie and empty beauty of the land, sky, and horizon erased, as if a gauzy white veil had dropped from the heavens with the mysterious purpose of obliterating all life on earth. Desperate to survive, a primal preservation instinct kicked in, and the hapless hunter unsheathed his large Bowie knife, ripping open the chest and belly of the buffalo. He slashed at the tangle of still warm and steaming innards, hauled out the bulk, wildly hurling it as far as he could, which was not very far. With deep foreboding, the panting and sweating man sucked in a lungful of the cold air, clutched his long coat tightly, and hurriedly tucked himself into the rib cage of the carved-out carcass to wait out the passing of the storm. A deep drift of windblown snow banked up on the back of the beast. The temperature continued to plunge, and soon, thick ice welded the rib cage in an unbreakable lock for the condemned man. Weeks later, as the frozen land thawed, the bison with the dead man embalmed inside was discovered. A grim picture of his final hour was evident by the contorted position of his body with hands interlaced through the ribs, as if he had tried to break through the cage using all the remaining strength he could muster. The ivory-handled Bowie knife, its leather sheath, and a rifle were liberated by the trapper who stumbled on the scene. Gravely crossing himself and mumbling a brief prayer, the trapper hastily buried the hunter's body in an unmarked grave. As the story unfurled, the goggled-eyed children, still innocent of the desperation adults are driven by, were riveted to the story teller as they hung on to every word, trying to imagine the madness of a man who sought refuge by sheltering in the gory carcass of a buffalo. A few of the adults recently arrived from back East found the story impossible to believe—but those that had survived the fury of a week-long blizzard in the foothills of the Rockies did not doubt the truth of the tale.

The more that Bass heard about various thwarted ruses to bring fugitives to justice, the greater grew his enthusiasm to employ his expertise. Few knew the terrain or the people who inhabited the Indian Nation as well as Bass. That he had lived among the tribes and survived the wild lands for nearly a decade was a testimony to his greatly admired skills, knowledge, and adaptability. On numerous occasions, Bass volunteered his services as a guide, accompanying agents and marshals on their missions into the Indian Territories to hunt and ferret out criminals. Bass found tracking fugitives and surprising them in their hideaways thoroughly thrilling and satisfying. Through the use of clever ploys and expert tracking skills, he successfully guided the Indian Police and federal marshals to clandestine ravines or water holes hidden by ten-foot high stands of cane that shielded a campsite or a temporary corral holding stolen horses.

His reputation for stealth and detection spread to Fort Smith, the headquarters for the minimal law enforcement in the Indian Territories. Lawyers and prosecutors shared confidential information with Bass, welcoming his opinion on current cases and trials. After dinner, the law men would often retire to the trellised porch of Bass and Jennie's home to continue spirited exchanges about the best way to entrap known fugitives from justice hiding in the Territories. Since there was little fear of legal retribution in the wild land across the river, homicides and crimes of violence were routine, with disputes swiftly settled by knife or by gun. Hunting down thieves and ruthless killers was highly dangerous work that offered little incentive for most of the peace-loving residents on the safe side of the Arkansas River.

In 1875, Judge Isaac Parker, the most feared of all federal judges, known as the "Hanging Judge," volunteered to offer his considerable experience to help bring law and order to the Indian Territories by serving as the judge in Fort Smith. Parker had already gained some fame as an advocate for tribal rights and supported the mission of the Bureau of Indian Affairs. He was committed to the idea of a smooth-running territorial government for the Indian Nation. More progressive than most, he also supported the rights of women to vote and to serve in political position in any of the Territories in the nation. He did not support the squatters or any of the eager settlers who lobbied Congress for a foothold in the land that had been lawfully assigned to the tribes.

Understanding that he would need the very best deputies and marshals to help him succeed in his mission of justice, he employed only the most fearless and skilled lawmen. Praise for Bass from his marshals captured the judge's attention. Bass's exceptional scouting abilities and mastery of the territories were skills the judge desperately needed in his goal to bring order and peace to the Territories. Judge Parker and his most trusted marshal extended an invitation to Bass to meet with them. Their admiration and respect for each other were mutual and immediate.

Bass Reeves, one of the very first African-American men west of the Mississippi River to hold the position of deputy marshal, was hired in 1875. With a fervent belief in the power of justice, Bass proudly accepted the opportunity to work with the famous and esteemed judge. The solemnity with which Bass pledged to execute the law without favor toward anyone impressed the judge, who knew he would be able to count on Bass in the momentous responsibility of ridding the Indian Nation of killers and thieves. Pinning the Deputy Marshal's badge on Bass's lapel was a decision Judge Parker never had cause to regret. Bass was aware that being appointed as a deputy marshal by Judge Parker and assigned to the Indian Nation, was unprecedented. It was both an honor and a confidence that Bass would never betray.

Chapter 8

Crossing the Dead Line and the
Court of the Damned

Initially appointed to the Utah Territory, Parker asked President Grant to nominate him to be the sole judge for the Western District of Arkansas, a court whose jurisdiction included the vast seventy four thousand square miles that made up the Indian Territories. When the scrupulously honest and highly respected Judge Parker volunteered for the thankless position of bringing law and discipline to the vast area that encompassed the Western District of Arkansas and the neighboring dangerous Indian Territories, President Grant gratefully accepted the offer. Parker would replace the previous federal judge, William Story, appointed by Ulysses Grant. Story had succeeded only in worsening the already difficult administration of the courts by feathering his own nest through deceit and trickery. Engaged in corrupt financial maneuvers, the notorious judge did nothing to prevent the rising surge in murders committed by blacks, Indians, and whites, who freely terrorized citizens and residents in the Indian Territories without fear of legal retaliation. The amount of money spent by his court was ten times more than his predecessor's expenditures. When the Congressional investigation charging Judge Story with findings of embezzlement, fraud, and undocumented expenditures of the court's money was published in the local newspaper, impeachment became imminent. Judge William Story packed his bags, left Arkansas, and hot-footed it to Colorado. He continued to expand his corrupt enterprises, opened a law firm, and invested in mining and railroads, among other interests. Though angry citizens in Van Buren questioned how the judge managed to escape justice and keep the ill-gotten money, nothing was done. The thriving enterprises and speculations that the corrupt Judge Story gambled on paid off, and he was free to lead a prosperous and influential life in his new home of Colorado, even serving later as Lieutenant Governor for Colorado in the early 1890s. The town of Van Buren regretted that Judge Story had never had to face his successor; the virtuous man who would have made sure justice was served.

Within weeks, Judge Parker's court, from which no appeals were granted for the next thirteen years, became known as the Court of the Damned, located on the very edge of the lawless territories fearfully identified as Hell's Fringe in later years. Word traveled swiftly through the Territories and both locals and outlaws referred to the miserable jail as Hell on the Border. An honest judge with a new and committed team of lawmen to enforce warrants, was a relief for the law-abiding townspeople. Merciless in his desire to rid the Indian Territory of outlaws, the thirty-six-year-old judge moved quickly with his objective to bring peace, security, and order to the area.

To the satisfaction of the local citizens, Judge Parker was tireless and devoted to his work. He tried more than ninety defendants in his first two months on duty, condemning eight to the gallows. One of the doomed convicts was shot in a futile attempt to escape the guards. The youthful years of another stirred the compassion of the Honorable Judge, who commuted his sentence to one of life imprisonment, but not before delivering an exhaustive commentary both to the public and to the misguided youth. One black man, three white men, and two Indians were charged with murder and convicted. All were sentenced to execution in accordance with the new federal law, passed after the Civil War, mandating execution for the crimes of rape and homicide. Charges were read aloud before the unforgiving rope was looped over their heads and circled their necks. A mob of more than five thousand residents and visitors gathered to witness the iron-fisted, long grasp of the law and gawk at the simultaneous hangings of six killers on the recently erected gallows beam. The famous gallows, nicknamed the Government Suspender, was a large and roughly hewn construction that stirred both awe and fear. With each execution, Judge Parker retired to a private room to offer prayers for the condemned and never witnessed a hanging.

Journalists from northern cities on the East Coast traveled great distances to record the shocking multiple executions. Capital punishment, viewed by many as immoral and cruel, evoked the same passionate debates that continued to rage far into the next two centuries, but, despite the outraged criticism of reporters far removed from the wild edge of the frontier, local citizens enthusiastically supported Judge Parker, who identified with the innocent victims of violent crime and harbored no sympathy for rapists or murderers. The controversial gallows that had 'suspended' eighty-six violent criminals would be shielded off from gawkers a few years later and then destroyed at the end of Judge Parker's tenure.

Word continued to spread throughout the territory and neighboring states that the new judge was a man to be reckoned with. Unlike his predecessor, Judge Parker could not be bribed nor did he permit appeals for those accused of capital crimes. The prospect of being tried in Fort Smith in the federal "Court of the Damned," under the gavel of the Hanging Judge, drove a spike of fear in the hearts of the most lawless of felons. Judge Parker's ambitious plan targeted the removal of all criminals hiding out in the Indian Territories. He further demanded the reopening of unsolved cases that had languished on the books during the crooked tenure of Judge Story. In the first court session of his service, Judge Parker tried eighteen men. Eight of the convicted prisoners charged with either murder or rape were mandated by the current law to be executed. Only six of the first convicted men were hanged. Fifteen more prisoners were convicted and given the death sentence that summer of 1876. The executions, open to the public, assured that Judge Parker's reputation as the Hanging

Judge who ruled the Court of the Damned spread with lightning speed to every miscreant holed up deep in the heart of the Indian Territories. The conservative judge was inflexible in his conviction that the subsequent trial, sentencing, and punishment of a criminal were powerfully effective deterrents to future crime.

Because Judge Parker was recognized as one of the first advocates for the rights of victims of violent crimes, and a staunch defender of tribal rights, reporters based in eastern cities tempered their comments with cautious respect. In a preview of yellow journalism, knowing that those who were proven guilty of rape, homicide, or treason faced capital punishment when convicted, the journalists sensationalized the expediency of frontier justice that allowed six murderers to be hanged simultaneously. That Judge Parker openly supported the view that the federally mandated law should be struck and the death penalty abolished was of much less interest to the urban readers in the East who preferred a more dastardly image of the prominent judge that conformed to the wild tales of the popular dime novels. When asked how he justified execution since he did not believe in the merits of capital punishment, Judge Parker famously responded, *I've never hanged a man. It is the law that has done it.* His job was to uphold the law, not make the laws.

Finally, in 1878, a high wood partition was erected around the gallows and the hangings were closed to the public. The newly fenced-off prison grounds doubled as a corral for cattle and horses between executions. Travelers passing through Fort Smith continued to be gruesomely attracted to the site of the scandalous "Government Suspender," the gallows from which criminals dangled after the executioner released the floor trap.

Only eighty miles west of Fort Smith, residents identified the border between western Arkansas and the stateless wild lands as the "Dead Line." No place out west was more dangerous than the Territories, which served as a lawless sanctuary for a swelling horde of cunning men and women, escaped convicts, and desperadoes of every kind. Whiskey runners and horse thieves staked out hideouts along hidden trails protected by carefully concealed surveillance points. Bands of craven killers and bank robbers, knowing that the law was unlikely to follow their trail, found illegal asylum in the hills and woods that nestled Indian villages.

With foresight and vigilance, Judge Parker selected two hundred resolute men to serve as officers and assigned them to the seventy-four thousand square miles of Indian Territory. Fugitives from justice from all states in the union hid safely in the wild and lawless country. The task was extremely formidable, the pay abysmal, and manhunts would necessarily absent the lawmen from their families for weeks at a time. Warrants were issued with the instruction to bring in criminals dead or alive. Parker, however, sought to avoid lawless shoot-outs in the Territories and, to minimize the chances of deputies taking the law into their own hands, they were to receive pay only for those criminals brought in alive. On rare occasions, a pair of boots and personal items might suffice as a substitute for a felon who died en route or was shot in self-defense by his captor. Although Parker was well aware that the sizable awards offered for the most dangerous felons tempted men of ambiguous character, the increasing number of heinous crimes in the Territories guided his decision to hire skilled gunmen, despite the somewhat shady backgrounds of a few. A few of the men the judge hired turned against the law; most notably, the Dalton brothers, who smuggled whiskey into the Territories, and, much later, joined the dangerous Doolin Gang, horse thieves, and murderers specializing in train robberies. Most of the men who worked for Judge Parker remained on the honest side of the law and worked tirelessly to bring order to the wild land.

Bass Reeves proved to be the most dedicated and intrepid of the men hired by Judge Parker. Familiar with Bass's reputation as an expert shooter, and impressed with his intelligence and idealism, the Judge knew he had found a trustworthy man who would meet the existing problems and those future ones that loomed ahead. Unlike some of the law officers, Bass was not driven by the rewards offered, nor was he biased against blacks, whites, or Native Americans. The same outrage at unfairness, that had driven him to knock out his card-cheating master so many years before, had grown into a passionate desire to rout out those who arrogantly flouted the law. His detective skills, coupled with his ability to communicate in the languages and dialects of the local tribes, was invaluable, as were the friendships with tribal chiefs and scouts that he made during his years as a fugitive. Despite an inability to read and write, Bass relied on ingenuity and memorization, serving warrants without error. Having spent nearly ten years living in the Territories as a fugitive himself, Bass was more familiar with the lay of the land and the hidden trails that crisscrossed through riverbeds and blackjack woods than were the outlaws who mastered only the terrain of relatively small areas. A longtime friend of many of the Freedmen who had married into the tribal communities, Bass had a supportive investigative network in place and his employer, Judge Parker, had earned the loyalty of the Indians who saw the judge as a protector of their rights to the land secured by treaties with the federal government.

Bass Reeves galloped into the swirling vortex of peril with the calmness and confidence that are characteristic of the truly courageous. And ride he did—on his gray stallion, Flint, sired by Magic, whose long silver mane, like a ghostly aura, shimmered with sparkles on moonlit nights. Wearing his trademark black hat, armed with a Winchester 73 and packing two .45 Colts, Bass was a formidable foe to enemies and a celebrated defender of the vulnerable. Bass appreciated the new developments in the manufacture of weapons after the Civil War that eliminated the need for different-sized ammunition, a welcomed convenience, and significant time saver. A master of clever disguises and ruses, a bemused smile often gave way to hearty laughter as Bass imagined novel strategies he would engage to hunt his man down.

Deep in his saddlebags, beneath the usual camping supplies necessary to survive in the wild frontier, Bass buried a mystifying assortment of accessories. Like an itinerant magician with a pocket of tricks, or a masked thespian auditioning for a performance, Bass was prepared to spin any illusion that convincingly concealed both purpose and identity. On a thin braided cord, a small deerskin pouch rested against his chest under his shirt. A gift from Chief Opothleyahola given to him years before; Bass treasured the tiny medicine bag that he knew, with surety, mysteriously shielded him from invisible dangers.

Chapter 9

Sunrise Surprise

It was late August when Bass took on the assignment to track down two brothers whose continual raids and successful disappearances frustrated deputies and residents of the Territories who had been victimized by them. Accused also of a homicide, the residents were eager for the murdering thieves to come face to face with Hanging Judge Parker. It was known that the brothers lived with their mother, a terrifying old harpy who could handle weapons as well as any outlaw and would not hesitate to shoot any intruder who stumbled across their unfenced property and would defend her sons to the death if needed. Her husband had abandoned her long ago, leaving her to raise the two unruly boys on her own in the Indian Nation. Full of bitterness and resentment, she feared her sons would also leave to seek their fortunes. Since a confrontation with either might result in their departure, she supported and encouraged them to engage in whatever deeds they deemed necessary without question, judgment, or nagging.

The blistering heat coupled with hot winds coated the land and brush with fine red dust. Autumn approached stealthily, robbing the green from the grass first, and yellowing the leaves of small trees. Lime-green nuts from the thirsty pecan trees pelted the children playing in the shade of the tall trees. The molted exoskeletons of cicadas littered the ground and the relentless thrumming of millions of male insects peaked and ebbed throughout the evenings. Mosquitoes dived hungrily at bared skin and chiggers competed for tender flesh underneath clothing. Sudden gusts of hot wind blew empty nests out of the trees, and the parched grass was sprinkled here and there with fallen leaves. Where there was no grass, cracks splintered the hard, dry earth. At sunrise, the plaintive cry of migrating geese overhead, as they flew south searching for water and food, cut through the morning stillness. The danger of wildfires was ever-present. Alarmed residents and travelers exchanged cautionary remarks. Those camping outside were scrupulous about fire safety and quickly doused any sparks leaping from their campfires. Makeshift windbreaks were constructed around the fires and canteens or buckets of creek water were readily on hand. Travelers exchanged stories of great fires far to the west; fires that raged for days and even weeks, fueled by incessant winds that hungrily devoured everything as the blazing inferno swept unhindered across the vast arid prairies. Magnificent sunsets tinged in violet glowed with orange and crimson hues; a celestial mirror reflected the burning land below.

Bass packed his gear, saddled Flint, and headed northeast from Muskogee early in the morning before daybreak. He wanted to cross the Arkansas River well before noon to join his posse near Tahlequah at the foothills of the Ozark Mountains in the Cherokee Nation. The wide river was lower than usual, allowing for easy navigation and a smooth crossing. Bass picked up a well-traveled trail on the other side. As he rode, he hummed softly. Every now and then, a smile peeked out from his bushy mustache as he thought about how he would trap the two horse-thieving killers. He amused himself by imagining himself disguised as an old woman wearing a blanket or a shawl. His height would betray him, and shaving his mustache was going beyond the pale, he laughed to himself. Or maybe, he could enlist Minewa's help and conceal himself in a bear hide and sneak up on the criminals. *Too dangerous, good chance I'd be shot by one of the brothers.*

The four men met Bass at the prearranged spot, a broad stand of cane a half mile east of one of the several mission schools that had been built a few years earlier. Charlie Birdwhistle, a Potawatomi guide who often rode with Bass, agreed to serve as camp cook and wagon driver, while Tuska-homa, now working with Bass, and Minewa were assigned as backup scouts. Otis Tucker, a free-lance posse man, also joined. The men loaded a creaking old wagon with tins and sacks of flour, dried beans, tobacco, and several jugs of honey before starting their journey further north where the bandit brothers were rumored to be holed up in a log cabin in a remote spot. The weather-beaten dilapidated wagon with rusted wheels and flaking paint was like that of any of the transient peddlers who plied their trade traveling slowly from village to village. The horse-drawn wagon, in fact, belonged to Charlie Birdwhistle's uncle and was often rented by Bass who had no desire to attract unwanted attention. Any sign of the law sniffing around was enough to send a lookout speeding back to the gang to sound the alarm. In an instant, the armed men would disperse, only to reunite days later at another well-concealed hideout.

Bass knew that his best bet was to get as close as possible without raising the suspicions of any casual passersby he would inevitably meet on the manhunt. Rolled up in Bass's deep vest pocket was the printed flyer offering a stupendous $5,000 reward for the live capture of both outlaws. A carefully sketched poster showed two sneering faces. In an effort to convey the defiance of the brothers, the artist had drawn them with heads tilted back, sharply highlighting their jutting chins and the missing front teeth of the older brother. Arched eyebrows accentuated the dark and menacing eyes that glared at the viewer. Bass wondered if the ragged scar that ripped across the left cheek of the older brother was a stroke of artistic license. At any rate, it was an unusually impressive illustration that Bass planned to add to his growing personal collection of official wanted notices and handwritten warnings posted on trees by both hunted outlaws and law officers. Though Bass was not usually motivated by reward money, $5000 was a powerful incentive.

The five men planned to spend the night at a small farm of an old friend. Rhett Ingram prepared a filling meal of roasted chicken and summer squash and the men talked long after sunset before Rhett led them to a nearby clearing. As they prepared to set up their camp, great sheets of lightning flashed unexpectedly and danced wildly across the rapidly darkening horizon. The distant rumbling of thunder far to the south, echoing across the valley, promised a long-awaited and much-needed rain. Transfixed by the dramatic panorama, Bass and his posse were silent as they gazed at the flashing sky crackling with electricity. The fresh smell of incoming rain with the sudden cooling air enervated the tired men. Tall cottonwood trees that edged the clearing, agitated by increasingly stronger winds, chattered incessantly and waved leafy arms, welcoming the approaching storm. Flint flared his nostrils and snorted excitedly. The other horses swiveled around and pawed the earth in eager anticipation of the approaching rain. Two sudden explosive cracks of thunder followed by a torrential downpour caused the horses to lurch up on their hind legs and sent the party racing back to the protective shelter of the roomy barn at the Ingram farm.

The storm passed during the night, and the recently rain-washed trees shimmered in the early morning mist. At dawn, Bass and his team repacked the wagon and waved goodbye to Rhett and his young daughter and son, who were studiously examining the hoof of one of the horses. Beneath a stack of woven blankets, burlap sacks, and reed mats, a thick coil of rope concealed a heavy box of padlocks and several sturdy chains. The four men agreed to meet later at another known campsite about thirty miles from the suspected hideout of the brothers. Charlie and Otis drove the wagon, while Minewa and Tuska-homa galloped off ahead. Bass twisted back and forth along the rough trail ahead of the wagon, dragging fallen branches off to the side and checking for mud holes and ruts that threatened to mire the wagon wheels.

Shortly after noon, Charlie and Otis came to a narrow but swollen river tributary. Bass was waiting for them and had already checked out a precarious bridge of rain-soaked planks that provided the only means to cross. The normally shallow creek had risen as high as its banks during the night and the rushing current carried fallen branches that clogged around the crudely made bridge supports. Flint gracefully navigated the rough water and scrambled up the muddy bank. Otis helped maneuver the derelict wagon without unfortunate incident across the slippery boards, as Charlie followed Bass's rapid hand signals.

A few hours later, Minewa and Tuska-homa met up with Charlie and Otis, who had set up camp and were chatting amicably with three Kickapoo traders headed north, their strong ponies loaded down with trade goods. Bass offered them tobacco and showed them the wanted poster of the two scowling men. With five fingers raised to indicate the number of hours by foot to the bandit's hideout, the youngest pointed toward the northeast. Bass and Minewa quizzed them about a rumored raid in the area. The three men excitedly confirmed that the two outlaws had recently made off with three fine horses and several weapons after partially burning down the front porch of the log cabin of Tunis Garrymore, a cantankerous, but respected old hunter and trapper who traded regularly with neighboring tribes. Tunis was checking his traps during the attack and it was thanks to his neighbors that the old man did not lose his cabin. Furious, Tunis was on a rampage and determined to seek revenge by lining up his own vigilante group. Bass sent a message via the young braves asking Garrymore to hold off for a few days.

Bass was up at dawn. Charlie Birdwhistle had set up a temporary make-do kitchen in the back of the wagon. Steaming coffee, bacon, and a towering stack of flapjacks were ready for the men. A pan of hot water, a shaving brush, and a small mirror rested against the trunk of a tree. Breaking his usual morning routine, Bass did not wash his face, shave, or trim his mustache before eating breakfast. Instead, he rummaged enthusiastically through supplies buried deep in the wagon. Humming in a low voice as was his habit, Bass worked on polishing up his disguise. The posse waited patiently for the character that would soon be revealed as they drank coffee and planned the hunting expedition which would occupy their day.

The man who suddenly appeared from the other side of the grove was only vaguely familiar. Gone were the snappy vest and crisp tall hat. In place of Bass Reeves, a slumped old man in ragged overalls, wearing a shabby hat with the brim partly shot off, limped into the campsite. The unkempt drifter with patched pant cuffs, a worn, woven bag slung over his shoulder, boots with missing heels, begged for a cup of coffee and breakfast, as his friends stared incredulously at the aged man before them. The disguise was perfect, and Bass was ready to start his thirty-mile hike through the open land. Bass embraced the role. Camouflaged as an elderly and limping hobo, he wished his companions a good day and slowly hobbled on in the direction pointed out to him by the Kickapoo traders.

It was a glorious morning for the long walk. Bass was careful not to allow his customary quick step to control his pace as he trudged along in the manner of an old man bent by time and ill fortune. Though not at all tired, he made sure to rest a few minutes every hour in case enemy scouts were secretly monitoring his approach. As an added touch, Bass whittled the twigs off a stout branch to serve as a cane. As Bass trekked through the brush and wild woods and waded across numerous creeks, he marveled at the untamed beauty of the land that innocently provided safe haven for so many desperadoes and felons. Stopping for a short rest in a shady grove, Bass snared a couple of hares and bagged them in one of the woven sacks he always carried. Having a gift to present to the brothers and the mother might lessen any suspicions they could have and ease his way into their trust.

Not long before dusk, Bass sighted the small log cabin he was searching for. As he neared the cabin, a wild-haired middle-aged woman fired two shots from her pistol and bellowed at him from her front porch. Placing his shot-up old hat on the end of his homemade cane, he waved to the squinting woman and shouted back that only yesterday he had escaped the grasp of the long arm of the law. So as not to arouse any suspicion, he sat down in the grass in full view and waited for her to welcome him into her home. As every sojourner knew, the unspoken code of hospitality in the remote and scarcely populated lands assured most journeyers of a meal, a wash-up, and a corner to bed down.

Verna Darrington, used to living in an isolated place, rarely communicated with others. Superstitious and suspicious of all who crossed her path, she trusted only herself and her two sons. She cared little that her boys were horse thieves and cattle rustlers, worrying only that they might be caught. That they were also rumored to have killed an itinerant peddler was certainly not her business, she felt. If the story should turn out to be true, Verna knew her boys would have had a good reason to kill someone, though, and of course, they would never get a fair trial and would have to face the Hanging Judge, an evil man who she believed would gladly hang her boys without reason on his famous Government Suspender. Verna, long hardened to an unforgiving and lonely life, spent her days chopping wood, mending fences, cleaning game, and honing her admirable shooting skills with both a pistol and a fine Remington rifle gifted to her by her eldest son. Devoted to her sons, Verna always kept a watchful eye for the law or nosy transients trespassing through the small spread, but, on this day, satisfied with his harmless and friendly demeanor, Verna Darrington invited the old drifter in for a meal and a chat. Perhaps he might have some useful gossip or share some important information that her sons would welcome about the conniving and underhanded lawmen constantly causing trouble and prying into everyone's business. *What business did lawmen even have in the stateless land? People could settle their own problems*, she muttered to herself.

Seeing her wave her arm as an invitation, Bass made sure to trudge slowly up to the porch as she watched him. Leaning his cane carefully against the railing of the front deck, he reached into the burlap bag slung over his shoulder and handed her the two hares. Startled at the unexpected gift of two recently caught rabbits from the old hobo, Verna nodded her thanks and, with a gesture, motioned him into the cabin and pointed to a straight-back wooden chair at the kitchen table. She poured Bass a cup of stout black coffee and slid a small jar of molasses across the table toward him. Verna suspected that the elderly old goat without a horse, limping along an overgrown trail in such a distant area, was probably suffering from the same softening of the brain that had erased her older brother's mind before he died a decade before. He too would wander around and approach any person he met. As they drank the black muddy coffee, Bass discretely studied her haggard appearance. Multiple cracks and creases bracketed her mouth and her deeply furrowed brow was etched into a permanent frown. The wiry scramble of untamed hair streaked with gray reminded Bass of an abandoned bird nest. A holstered pistol rested on her left hip. He assumed it was loaded. Her frequent habit of rapid blinking and squinting alerted Bass to her poor eyesight. *She's tougher than an Apache's tomahawk,* Bass observed, *this old mother of two outlaw sons. Better keep an eye on her.*

Bass, thoroughly enjoying his role, fabricated an entertaining tale detailing his narrow escape from one of Hanging Judge Parker's newly employed, feebleminded marshals. The law officer had stupidly shot at the hat that he had waved temptingly from the tip of his cane as he hid in a thicket, a standard trick that rarely failed to deceive a greenhorn. His frightened old horse had bolted, leaving him to travel shamefully and slowly on foot. Verna commiserated with the elderly man as she worked over the stove preparing dinner. Together, they cursed Hanging Judge Parker and his pack of unhinged marshals and lawmen that were always causing needless grief by interfering in the lives of folks in the Territories. They agreed that federal agents from across the Arkansas River had no business in the free and stateless land. They shared their mutual observation that the people from "the States", who came mucking around in the Indian Nation, could not be trusted, particularly the sneaky squatters slinking in across the Kansas border who lusted for the stateless land to become part of the Union. That would really be a devastating turn of events, should that ever happen, and she and her boys would have to pack it up and move on to the Arizona or New Mexico Territories where they could live as they wanted without the law hanging over them. After an hour of conversation, Verna reconsidered her initial assessment of Bass. He was a harmless old vagabond afflicted with arthritis, poor hearing, slow speech, and a limp, but there were no indications of mental derangement.

A sharp long whistle followed by two short pinging sounds brought Verna instantly to the front of the house. She motioned Bass to join her on the porch also. About a quarter of a mile away, two mounted men fired into the sky and Verna walked towards them. As an added precaution, Bass stepped off the porch and made it a point to lean wearily on his knotty old cane, scanning the skies as innocently as any farmer searching for a lone rain cloud. An animated talk, judging by the gestures and rising voices, followed. Apparently assured by their mother that the stranger threatened no danger, was on foot, and had even brought a gift, the brothers dismounted and walked their horses to a small corral to the east of the house. They nodded reassuringly to Bass as if to squelch any anxiety the old horseless geezer might have. Bass touched his worn hat in gratitude for their acceptance of him and continued to calmly stare at the sky until they returned from the corral and invited him back into their home.

Dinner was typical fare of potatoes, biscuits, and grilled buffalo meat. The men ate heartily, exchanging stories and cursing the lawmen and their cunning Indian scouts who ranged through the Territories, betraying all those who simply wanted to live their own lives and were quite capable of taking care of their own troubles and solving any disputes that should arise. There was no need for the courts in Arkansas, Texas, or anywhere to intervene in the business of the residents of the Indian Territories. They agreed with their mother that, should the old Indian Nation ever become a state, they would relocate to any stateless territory that survived the relentless forces that threatened to choke off their freedom with the cruel yoke of 'statehood'.

The brothers recounted their latest escapade. They chortled over the high prices they had finagled with a dealer from across the border in Texas for three strong stallions stolen from a wily old trapper over near the Kickapoo land. Eluding the law was their specialty, and they commended the unexpected visitor on successfully outwitting a marshal who worked for Hanging Judge Parker. To escape from the maw of the Arkansas law was to be saved from a certain death sentence. Bass vigorously agreed as the brothers served themselves another round of meat and biscuits. Bass noticed that Verna, now completely at ease, had removed her holster and hung it on an iron hook over a small corner cabinet next to the table. With both sons at home, she did not need to worry about protection. Their easy conversation and raucous laughter were a clear sign that her boys trusted the bedraggled old vagabond.

Bass knew that rumors of hidden, abandoned, or buried treasure of gold and silver were never disregarded and always commanded rapt attentiveness. To further win their trust, he rattled off a convincing tale about a stash of gold and silver coins he had thought prudent to hide in the

Gloss Mountains much further west in the Cherokee Outlet the year before on his return trip from prospecting at the Golden Fleece mine in Colorado. Bass elaborated on his misfortunes. Unfortunately, he had not been able to return as quickly as he planned because his aging and widowed mother in Missouri had taken a bad turn of health. Bass sighed as he recounted their last loving encounter and her peaceful death. He shrugged his shoulders at the mysterious tangles and ill-starred twists of life. Verna listened attentively and nodded in approval that he had temporarily forsaken such a valuable treasure to visit his old and ailing mother. As she cleared the table, she wondered briefly if her sons would do the same for her. She doubted it but repressed the unpleasant thought.

It was then that Bass suggested that they join up together to better their chances to retrieve the hidden gold stashed in a deep crevice blocked by two sizable rocks. He explained that he was suffering from the cursed pains of old age and needed two younger fellows to travel with him through the dangerous and uncivilized region to recover the secret trove, which he would gladly split with them. In fact, he was on his way west when the unfortunate run-in with the law usurped his plans. He was sure he would have no trouble borrowing a mule or a horse from an old miner friend who lived further west and the boys could catch up with him a few days later.

The unsuspecting brothers exchanged sly winks and promised to accompany the accursed old man who had obviously fallen on hard times since his early gold mining days in the San Juan Mountains in Colorado. They agreed to make detailed plans in the morning about where to meet after a good sleep. To seal the new alliance, the brothers toasted each other and offered Bass a shot of bootlegged whiskey smuggled into the Territories from their recent Texas run. Bass enthusiastically agreed and toasted his new friends. He embraced the role, and Verna joined her sons for their third tumbler of firewater just as Bass reached across the table, carelessly knocking his cup and splashing out the unwanted liquor. The brothers glanced quickly at each other and laughed at the clumsy old man who certainly could not even fire a straight shot and would be an easy mark to take out later after liberating the hidden loot. His stumbling manner and halting explanation, punctuated with coughs and sighs persuaded them to believe his story. There were as many tales about treasures lost due to theft or death as there were about fortunate discoveries of hidden loot that had never been recovered, and the story the old man told was as conceivable as any.

Bidding them goodnight, Bass moved towards the front door as if to sleep on the porch, but the unsuspecting brothers suggested that the weak and ailing old man share their room after one more drink. The intoxicated brothers, slurring and stumbling, bedded down next to each other, and Bass unrolled his pad a polite distance from them. Verna retired to the second bedroom on the other side of the log cabin. As he waited for the alcohol to anesthetize his prey, Bass exhaled loudly and turned his back to the brothers. He feigned a deep sleep by adding several phlegmy snorts and convincing moans. Within minutes, the two brothers fell into a leaden slumber. The silence in the cabin was broken with sudden gasping groans and grinding teeth. Bass did not delay long before reaching deep into his faded woven bag, his nimble fingers searching for the familiar feel of thick metal rings.

The brothers never moved as Bass handcuffed their limp wrists together. Bass emptied their guns, tucking the unused ammunition into his bag, and slipped stealthily into the central room where he also emptied the double-barreled shotgun that stood like a sentry against the door. He hid Verna's pistol in a crockery pot that sat on the cabinet shelf. *She'll probably need it later when she's alone*, Bass thought. Rearranging his worn blanket, Bass fell peacefully asleep and awoke just as the pale light of dawn crept into the room. He calmly assessed the two grimy men who had fallen asleep still wearing their boots and smiled before waking them with a brusque shake of their shoulders. The brothers woke slowly, moaning and squinting in the dim light. Only as they tried to stretch the stiffness out of their arms and legs, did they realize they were shackled together.

As he led the screaming, cuffed men out into the yard, Verna came storming out the front door screeching and wailing as she grabbed for the emptied shotgun, aiming it at Bass who walked calmly behind the two brothers. Every now and then, he twirled a small revolver that he had tucked in an inside pocket of his baggy worn overalls. Verna followed Bass and her condemned sons for three miles before giving up the chase. Bass felt a tinge of regret at having outsmarted the fierce mother who had failed to save her boys from the law and was now faced with surviving entirely on her own in the dangerous land. He was glad he had not taken her pistol which she would surely find later. For many miles, the shackled men, still suffering from the effects of their bootlegged whiskey, continued to curse and howled out a string of bitter oaths promising revenge.

"Sunrise surprise, boys," Bass's voice boomed, "Time to say goodbye." It had been a successful mission and Bass felt good.

As the prisoners wearily trudged on, Bass delivered a spirited monologue sprinkled with an abundance of rhetorical questions about honesty and justice to his captive audience of two. After his brief sermon, Bass was moved to sing the increasingly popular hymn written by a Choctaw freedman less than two decades before, a further annoyance to the two criminals. Bass liked that the freedman, Wallis Willis, was inspired by the beauty and serenity of the Red Rive,r which reminded him of the biblical River Jordon, when he first composed *Swing Low, Sweet Chariot*. As he neared the campsite, Bass changed tunes and Otis and Minewa heard Bass bellowing out one of his favorite frontier ballads. They knew the boss had been victorious once again. Minewa was anxious to relay the good news to Tunis Garrymore that the thieves had been arrested.

Chapter 10

Famous Escapades

Bass rarely made the long trip back to Fort Smith from deep in the Indian Territories without a string of chained men in tow. Law-abiding citizens were thrilled to the spectacle of Bass and his posse riding through town leading a wagon full of men chained together. Bass's reputation soared as stories of amazing feats traveled by word of mouth throughout the Territories and back to the civilized towns east of Hell's Fringe. On his arrival at Judge Parker's court, a new stack of warrants was ready for Bass to have read to him so that he could commit the particulars to memory.

A well-earned respite at home with Jennie and his boisterous children was often interrupted by another urgent assignment necessitating an immediate return to the Territories. Jackson Longarm had built a small cabin next to the Reeves's two-story farmhouse. This allowed him to keep a protective watch over his daughter and grandchildren and help care for the stock and farm; an arrangement that satisfied all. After Bass had completed his business in Fort Smith, he would go home and regale the family with tales of the perilous life across the border.

Many of the stories he told were humorous and sympathetic as he carefully avoided alarming his wife and children. Bass never detailed the gruesome crimes and dangerous circumstances for his captive listeners that preceded a successful capture. His family was well aware of his fame as a law officer who always caught his man, and they preferred to hear about curious tribal customs and the ordinary travails of the inhabitants of the Territories.

When prodded by a knowing guest, Bass would launch into a wildly dramatized reenactment of an escapade that had reached the ears of those on the safe side of Hell's Fringe. As often as not, the adventures he recounted had to do with confronting nature and ingenious means of survival that he had learned throughout his many years in the Indian Nations.

One of the stories that never failed to entertain was the tale of Bass coming across a group of careless young cowboys who were trying to rescue a huge copper-colored longhorn mired in a mud bar at the Canadian River. The lasso tightened with every frenzied move, strangling the poor animal, whose massive body was sinking rapidly in the treacherous sludge. In a flash, Bass stripped down, waded into the thick muck, and grabbed the head and horns of the choking beast to loosen the taut rope around its muscular neck. Struggling to keep his balance against the swirling current, he dug his heels into the slippery clay and jerked the mighty straining head sharply backward. The panicked creature inhaled deeply and noisily, his heaving chest rising from the sludge just long enough for Bass to hoist up his mud-locked front legs. As Bass told the story, the stressed bull gazed at Bass, his grateful eyes gleaming with the sure knowledge of freedom, and, with a sudden mad twist, the river surrendered its hold with an explosive-sucking slurp. With a thunderous snort, the longhorn shook his head as he dragged himself out of the deadly ooze and gained a firm foothold on the sandy bank. Within moments, he scrambled up the bank and was out of sight.

Bass eased himself back to the shore where the dumbfounded green-horn cowboys gaped as he scraped off great clods of gummy clay from his thighs and hips before he mounted Flint. The bewildered cowboys watched with dumbfounded amazement when Bass attached his muddy boots to the saddle horn of his horse. After bundling and stuffing all of his clothes in his capacious saddlebag, Bass wheeled Flint around in a swooping arc and tipped his hat, the only piece of clothing he wore. Silhouetted against the fiery sunset, the splendid sight of the dark naked man, barefoot and wearing only his hat, astride his sterling steed further astounded the boys, who recovered their lost voices and whistled as Bass galloped off. Bass followed the crest of the riverbank until he could no longer hear their wild cheers. Further upstream, Bass bathed and dressed before setting up camp for the night several miles from the troublesome tenderfoots. Bass settled onto his blanket and searched the sky for familiar constellations that Minewa had pointed out for him so long ago. It was the middle of August and, ever since childhood, Bass had always looked forward to the annual display of streaking stars arcing overhead on clear dark summer nights. The silence and ethereal beauty of thousands of winking sparks intercepted by long star streaks dazzled Bass who fell into a deep and peaceful sleep.

One of the most favored and gripping stories that held the attention of the neighbors who gathered at the Reeves's home was the story of how Bass had rescued a young Potawatomi mother and her infant son during a blinding blizzard two winters before.

On a late January afternoon, angry wailing winds whipped the swirling snow in deep drifts. As the blizzard intensified, the horizon vanished behind the deathly white shroud that now veiled all familiar signs of humanity. The heavily snow-laden boughs of great trees, their skeletal fingers dressed in icy gloves, cracked under the weight of the rapidly freezing snow. Furious winds screamed through the cedar hollow where Bass and Flint hunkered down against a massive drift to wait out the worst. Finally, the violent winds roared on towards the open plains out west, leaving an unearthly stillness behind. A curtain of snow continued to drift from the heavens. Bass loosened the wool scarf Jenny had knitted for him and reflected on the ethereal beauty of the silent scene. The chilling winds reached a crescendo and then the ear-piercing whistling subsided. Flint was the first to hear the sound of approaching danger. He scrambled up abruptly with his neck extended and nostrils quivering in the rarefied air. Alerted, Bass listened closely. Yes, it was the frenzied howling of a pack of starving wolves moving in on their target. The pack was not far off. In a fast moment, Bass brushed the snow off Flint and quickly mounted him. Like the fabled celestial centaur, man and horse stood as one creature, sniffing the air as they listened to the increasingly sharp yelps of the wild beasts closing in on their victim. The screech of the young woman sent a chill through Bass. He knew without doubt that she carried an infant whose lips smelled of sweet, warm, human milk. The subtle smack of Bass's quirt sped Flint through the veil of falling snow towards the ravenous wolves. As the living centaur approached the edge of the circling beasts, Bass saw the woman crouched in a snow bank. She clutched her infant to her chest, screaming in terror, as the emaciated wolves formed an ever-narrowing ring. Bass aimed and fired at the snarling leader, whose contorted body twisted as he collapsed. Crazed by their hunger, the five remaining wolves twitched and jerked, but did not bolt when the sharp crack of Bass's rifle shattered the silence. They crept closer and closer towards the hysterical woman who now lay face down on the snow bank, her baby beneath her panting breast. With lightning speed and a pistol in each hand, Bass brought down the pack and, within seconds, the grisly slaughter of the animals was over. As Bass enfolded the stricken woman with her whimpering child into his arms, he grimaced at the evidence of violence. Like plum juice spilled on a pristine white tablecloth, the dark blood of six carcasses stained the virginal snow.

Bass mounted Flint and secured the distraught woman and her wailing child in front of him before riding through the snow banks back to the safety of the village. Clutching her baby to her breast, the young woman, Itajawee, knew that the Great Spirit had answered her desperate prayers. That night, the grateful villagers shared their meager reserve, and Bass was treated to grilled onions and venison with hot cornbread soaked in molasses. Two young braves returned to the kill site to skin the wolves. The stiffening carcasses, powdered with snow, formed an unnatural mound at the base of the tree. With swift expertise, the young warriors stripped the skin from the wolves, stacked the raw pelts and skinned carcasses on a makeshift sled of cedar branches, and dragged the heavy load back to the tanning hut. Far into the night, the group feasted around a campfire that blazed and crackled as the bitterly cold gusts of wind teased the licks of flame. They told stories of dangerous wanted outlaws that remained on the run in the Indian Lands.

Ned Christie was a controversial figure much discussed. Ned was a proud Cherokee with a great allegiance toward his tribe and a deep suspicion of the white men who were slowly but steadily gaining an increasingly large foothold in the lands set aside for his people through past treaties. Known as a deadeye shot, a talented blacksmith, and an articulate spokesperson for the tribe, he was treated with deference by both neighbors and friends. Also active in territory politics, Ned served as a Cherokee senator in the local government of the tribe. Attractive, wild-spirited, smart, and strong, Ned was feared by many of the marshals and respected by some of the tribal communities. Ned hated the snaking railway network that encroached ever more on Indian lands. He loathed the ongoing devious plans that aimed to dissolve the communal lands reserved for the Cherokees by dividing the vast tracks into allotments, thereby promoting interest in individual property rights, *another ruse to steal our land and kill our spirit,* he explained to the less informed of his people. When the famed Cherokee Female Seminary, an institute of pride and progress, one of the few places a young woman could get an education, burned to the ground in a devastating fire, Ned attended the council to investigate and discuss the tragedy. On the same evening that Ned sped to Tahlequah, the capital of the Cherokee Nation, a US Marshal was murdered in the area. Ned had many enemies and, when he was falsely accused of the crime by an unidentified witness, he was charged and arrested by the outraged deputy marshal of the man killed. His efforts to convince the law officer of his innocence in the crime were not successful and Ned was ordered to appear before Judge Parker in Arkansas. Not trusting the court to defend him, he refused to show up and fled deep into the Territories, where his loyal friends gladly offered protection and help. Ned was able to elude capture and conceal his hideaway for several years. A warrant for his arrest was always included in the stash of writs Bass carried. Five years later, Bass and his posse discovered his cabin hidden in the woods, and, hoping to flush him out, they set fire to the roof. Ned managed to escape and, with the steadfast support of his network of devoted companions and his knowledge of the land, he continued to evade arrest. Over the next couple of years, his notoriety grew, with even his enemies grudgingly acknowledging his prowess at slipping past the law. Ned rebuilt a fortified home and remained free for several more years until Judge Parker's marshals finally caught up with him. By now, the list of violent crimes he was accused of defied imagination. It seemed as if every theft, rape, or plunder was initiated or caused by Ned Christie. Until his death by gun sometime later, he was one of the most wanted outlaws in the Territories. Whether the handsome Ned Christie was a brave warrior who defended the sovereignty of his people, or a subversive rebel who chose to fight the inevitable changes that swept across the old Indian Nation, was a topic hotly debated by both friends and enemies long after his death. Two decades later, Ned Christie's name was cleared when a witness to the crime finally spoke out, but the belated revelation was celebrated by only the few who still remembered those dark days.

The gathering of tribal members shared stories of courageous deeds and miraculous interventions. They lowered their voices when they talked about the long, dark shadow cast by the advancing tide of intruders. They knew with sickening surety, baring a miracle from the Great Spirit, that the tidal wave of pioneers and settlers would eventually invalidate existing treaties and promises with clever deceptions and tricks and would succeed in stealing their designated land, their own promised Indian Nation.

Itajawee's father talked about mysterious signs and vivid dreams that bespoke of ominous events to come. A darkly disturbing dream he had had as a young brave continued to haunt him throughout his life and, now, with the wisdom that only the passage of time or great suffering can bring, he understood with crystal clarity the dream's prophesy. It was a dream announcing the inevitable future and offered no solution. In the vision, representatives of many tribes gathered in a dense forest. Strangely, ancient tribal animosities and divisiveness had evaporated and all stood in silent unity around a tree of such beauty and strength that no song or musical instrument could express its splendor. Birds and insects of every size and hue flitted among the leafy branches that glowed in the light of the setting sun. A lone cloud drifted by and soft gusts fluttered through the iridescent leaves. Quivering, winged insects were the first to abandon the ancient tree. Within moments, the sky grew darker and the whispery breeze steadily increased and grew stronger. First one, and then a sprinkle of leaves floated slowly to the ground. The twisting and spiraling leaves danced their own enigmatic ballet as they drifted ever faster to the earth. The wind increased and a mysterious hum interrupted the silence, causing the strangely colorful birds to take wing. Within moments, a rainbow of plumage vanished out of sight and over the horizon. The whirring noise grew to a wail as the now swirling leaves, ripped off by an invisible force, twisted crazily in the air. Within minutes, the weeping tree stood naked and leafless. Slowly, the trunk sucked in the branches until only a single enormous spike rose from the ground. And then… that last bare remnant of the glorious tree began to heave and contract, leaving only a wormy and blackened stump.

The terrifying dream, shared with the shaman and the tribe, was never forgotten. The ominous warning of Itajawee's father's sad vision of loss was chilling, and, day by day, the truth of the prophetical dream was evident. Game was meager and the majestic herds of buffalo nearly eradicated. The mass killings by heartless entertainment seekers of the beloved givers of life were akin to sharpened blades piercing through each and every heart of every individual tribal member. Power, dignity, and sustenance were soon to be totally vanquished, and the surviving people would join the ghosts of those who already inhabited the land of past memories. Throughout the so-called "Indian Nation", the tribes were suffering not only from scarcity of food and fuel, but also the painful and humiliating loss of their lands, language, and culture. With the disappearance of the buffalo, the great soaring bald eagles which had fed on the carrion as they sailed through the territory in the late autumn months, had vanished. To see two hundred magnificent birds roosting in the tall trees that bordered the rivers was a memory of their parents. Symbols of freedom and power, the sighting of wintering eagles winging their way south had always been a sign of blessings to come. Menacing and heartbreaking, the signs of a climactic shift in the balance of power were obvious to anyone who had the ears to hear, the eyes to see, and the heart to feel.

The crucible fed by the wild frontier and wealthy developers was in the process of melding, securing, and taming powerful forces that disdained the rights or culture of the original inhabitants. A deepening feeling of hopelessness and great despair washed through the tribal communities with the realization that no miracle would save them. Loss of respect, faith, and life would erase their existence, ancient culture, and, in time, even, memories would evaporate.

Itajawee's uncle, Chief Two Moons, stoked up his clay pipe and reminded the hushed circle about the tragedy of three springs before. The infant boy, Little Fox, less than a month old, had vanished from the homemade woven cloth cradle the mother had knotted to a low branch on a cottonwood tree that grew just beyond the blackberry bushes bordering the riverbank. The young mother, concentrating on her search for tender new roots and spring buds for her infant child, had wandered a short distance from the sleeping child, peacefully swinging in the small cloth hammock that the resourceful woman had fashioned. So absorbed was she in collecting the delicate young shoots that peeked from under the decaying leaves, she never noticed the gradually descending shadow of a wondrously large golden eagle. As if breaking against an invisible barrier in the air, the eagle's golden razor-sharp talons extended. With one powerful grasp, the emperor of the sky seized the week-old infant, no heavier than a wild hare. There must have been a rustle of wings, a squawk, a ripping sound of fabric, or perhaps, it was her mother's intuition. In that last moment of peace, unaware that her sanity was about to spiral into utter despair, she sang a lullaby her grandmother had taught her. Trusting in the eternal protection of the Great Spirit, the innocent woman casually turned her head to check on her firstborn.

The group around the campfire humbly pondered nature's awesome power. What should be revered more than the Great Spirit, a power that could deliver anguish and suffering, as well as bounty and wealth? As if hypnotized, the low-pitched chant that rose from the women mesmerized Bass, and he settled languidly against a heap of hides. The women silhouetted against flashing flames swayed in unison. Old men, with the young braves following, began drumming a beat that seemed to mimic the random pattern of the sparking flames. Behind the circle of adults, the children rattled dried gourds in a mesmerizing rhythm. The women continued to chant in unison. The shared lamentation, as if issuing from one being, transported its damaged and fearful audience to a world of safety, unity, and serenity. The haunting mourning song ended shrilly with an unexpectedly piercing note that shattered the ethereal-like trance of the listeners, plunging them unmercifully back into a bitter world blanketed in ice and snow.

Bass was a kind and thoughtful man and on that fearful night he considered his destiny. Always aware of that twisting two-headed dragon that steered his life, twin brothers who quested both adventure and justice, Bass knew he was compelled to chase the wild and buckling destiny that the lawless lands heaved at him. He gently tapped the small medicine bag that he wore under his shirt. Although Bass was not overly superstitious, he believed that the mysterious forces that guided events were unpredictable, powerful and ever-present. Not respecting or honoring the Great Spirit or the god of the Christians invited adversity and misfortune. *Maybe the Christian Lord and the Great Spirit are one and the same,* Bass thought, but *in different disguise, assuring a welcome by all.*

He recalled the time when he had to serve a writ to a Seminole medicine man, Yah-Kee, who aided Seminole horse thieves by providing an expensive mysterious potion that Yah-Kee claimed would protect them from the grasp of the law. It did not take Bass and his men long to find and arrest Yah-Kee and the two lawbreaking thieves. Bass and Minewa brought the three surly prisoners back to the camp to be watched over by his posse. After shackling the men together, Bass felt a strange shudder run through his spine and down his legs. Weakness overcame him and, unable to stand without trembling, he leaned against the scarred bark of a pine tree near the wagon. Yah-Kee's black eyes stared unblinkingly at him. Bass believed without a doubt that he was under a powerful and cursed spell. Gathering all of his remaining strength in one lunge, he tore the small leather pouch off of Yak-Kee's neck and hurled it into the smoldering fire. Bright violet flares spewing strange star-shaped sparks suddenly shot three feet up from the embers. As if answering a call from the spirit world, Minewa immediately started chanting in a low-pitched voice while Yah-Kee howled and begged Bass to retrieve the pouch before the fire consumed it. As the violet flame continued to burn and the color darkened to a deep purple, Bass felt strength and balance returning. Yah-Kee crumpled into a fetal position and refused to utter another word on the long journey to Arkansas. Bass, fully restored from the mysterious affliction and humbled by the experience, never again questioned the mystical powers of the supernatural or the spirit world.

Only two weeks before, Bass had been given another secret blend of herbs crushed to a fine powder. He was instructed to thicken it with his own saliva into a paste to be applied on any gunshot or knife wound or the deadly bite of a rattler. Bass welcomed the gift that promised protection from treachery or physical harm and stashed the valuable medicine in another one of his many hidden pockets. As he drifted off to sleep, he thanked the potent magic of the herbal blend that had already saved him more than a few times from harm.

Years later, when Bass was charged with having killed his own chuck wagon cook while out on a lengthy assignment, he was acquitted when the circumstances were detailed and supported. Bass's great love of dogs could tolerate no cruelty or maltreatment of the loyal animals. When the transient cook who was substituting for Charlie Birdwhistle at his camp violently kicked and then, in a fit of blind rage, threw a skillet of hot grease on Ajax, his beloved hunting dog, Bass, in one of his rare blasts of anger, shot at the ground near the cook's foot, inadvertently causing him to stumble into the fire pit and fatally crack his head on the sharp rocks that circled the pit. Minewa took off at a gallop to find a doctor and the cook was made as comfortable as possible. Unable to save the chef, Bass was charged with inadvertent homicide. Bass turned himself in and was duly arrested. The bond was a hefty three thousand dollars. Bass was able to cover the huge sum and hired a lawyer. Bass's financial reserves were greatly depleted and he never recovered the wealth he and Jennie had so painstakingly saved. The distraught posse, called in to testify, concurred that they had witnessed the cruelty and the ensuing unfortunate accident and that Bass had not intended to kill the cook. Bass was acquitted by Judge Parker on the basis of a weapon malfunction. Days later, Bass confided to Jennie that he attributed the just acquittal to the powerful promise of the charmed pouch to protect him in all difficult circumstances.

Chapter 11

Famous Arrests and Close Calls

Judge Parker, fully trusting in the skills of his favored marshal, often sent Bass on assignments that would challenge many of the other marshals. Of all the outlaws that Bass had tracked and shackled to bring back to Judge Parker, he was most self-satisfied with his wily success in liberating the Cherokee Nation of the famed outlaw, Bob Dozier. Bob Dozier had succeeded in evading capture for his odious deeds by working as a lone wolf. Never associated with any gang or partners, he operated on his own and managed his criminal activities as a kind of business. Not one to stick with one trackable crime, Bob Dozier engaged in a multitude of diverse dealings, specializing in all. Though a successful farmer early in his life, endless days of mending fences, taking care of his few cattle, plowing his small acreage, watching for signs of changing weather, harvesting, and selling the meager crops he harvested, began to weary him. When his pregnant young wife was bitten by a rattler and drowned in the cattle pond, he lost all interest in his small farm. As he hauled water from his well and repaired a gate, a few months after his wife's untimely death, Bob realized that the routine and daily chores no longer satisfied. Still a young man, now alone, he saw no reason to settle for the tough and hard life of a trader, a miner, or a farmer, dealing daily with only matters of physical survival. Investing, gambling, or detective work would be far more intriguing, but the first required funds, the second luck, and the third, training, none of which he had. It did not take Bob Dozier much time to conclude that his considerable talent was being wasted behind the mule and plow and that a satisfying future called for risk, pleasure, and, most importantly, a more lucrative profession assuring more income and less labor.

Dozier envied the saucy and wanton ways of the drifters and outlaws he ran into in the Territories. The excitement of unpredictable events and the danger of a life outside the law captivated him; all activities that were illegal offered thrilling invitations, stimulating games requiring cleverness, and the rewarding opportunity of outwitting others. Humility was not a characteristic Dozier was familiar with and, confident that he was surely as sly as anyone, Dozier drank a couple of shots of bootlegged whiskey and considered his best options. Congratulating himself on his intelligence and boldness, he allowed himself another short snort. An unexpected intoxicating thrill surged through him. *"I'll be dozin' no more,"* he laughed uproariously and fired his rifle at the stars above. Dozier was about to be unleashed.

Dozier's long list of preferred illegal activities included bank robberies, theft and resale of horses and cattle, and smuggling weapons and alcohol to any buyer who had the cash or offered a profitable trade. Bob much preferred to work alone. A shrewd land swindle or a successfully conned game of cards only added fuel to his glee at outwitting his victims. As crimes piled up, Dozier became more ruthless and arrogant. Giddy from his new power that stirred fear in everyone he met, and his numerous successful crimes, he no longer hesitated to kill anyone who stood in his way and his infamous reputation spread throughout the Creek and the Cherokee Nations. Because of his clever ploys and illusiveness, Bob Dozier, like a camouflaged rattlesnake or bobcat in the grass, remained unseen, feared, and free to carry on with his profitable but risky career. Confident that he could steal a march on any lawman, Dozier spent little time worrying about an arrest. Terrified of ever having to confront Dozier, people were silent when questioned by the Lighthorse Policemen of the Territories or any authority responsible for reporting or bringing outlaws to justice. This fear worked only to Bob Dozier's advantage, allowing him to expand his area of rampages and conquests. Why he had waited so long to live a life of freedom and adventure baffled him.

Bass was determined to arrest him and haul him to Judge Parker, who would reward the prisoner with his deserved punishment. For months, Bass hung back and checked every lead as to the whereabouts of Dozier. Bass was unruffled and sure of eventual success. Dozier caught the drift of rumors that Bass, the most feared of lawmen who worked for Hanging Judge Parker, was sniffing his trail and circling in. Dozier had no doubt he could outwit the famed lawman and smirked at the thought of a faceoff, with a fatal shootout ending in his favor.

It was a cloudy, rainy day and Bass was scanning a well-worn path to pick up the trail from Dozier, who had just sold a wagonload of bootlegged liquor from Arkansas to a small band of cattle rustlers. Bass had arrested three of the thieves, who were now shackled to a cedar tree near Bass's camp, and, as usual, were guarded by the vigilant eyes of his posse. Bass's main sidekick, Minewa, followed close behind. Dark clouds continued to gather, thunder rumbled far away, and the sky grew darker. Sheet lightning flashed on the horizon and the sudden booming cracks of thunder startled the snorting horses. The constantly flickering blue and white lights on the horizon gave way to dramatic flashes of blinding lightning that illuminated the trees and hills in ghastly relief. Trees swayed, dead branches crashed to the ground as heavy rain fell, flooding the already slippery trail, and erasing tracks.

Bass and Minewa ducked for cover and headed down a rocky ravine bordered by scrub oak and blackjack trees. As the horses skidded down the slippery slide of mud, a bullet whizzed by Bass and embedded itself in a nearby tree trunk. As if mortally wounded, Bass tumbled off Flint and lay low, waiting under a scrabble of trees. Lightning flashed, revealing a ghostly scene. Bass slowly pulled out his Colt.45, positioned it on the crook of his right arm, cocked it, and waited, ready to fire at the slightest hint of movement. His patience rewarded him and he watched as Dozier crept through the slippery sludge toward him. Dozier was sure he had, at the very least, winged the famed marshal in the shoulder. Slowly, inch by cautious inch, Dozier eased toward the copse of trees, a snake in the mud silently slithering toward Bass. Bass did not move a muscle and waited patiently as his predator slowly slunk ever nearer. Chortling gleefully, Dozier now suspected that his bullet had hit the mark and Bass Reeves, if not dead, was fatally wounded. He wormed his way ever closer and, when he was about four yards away, Bass released the trigger sending Dozier on to Glory Land with one blast. Dozier was no more. That the age-old trick of playing possum would have caused his own demise is not something Dozier would have been proud of.

Dozier was one of the fourteen men that Bass killed in the line of duty. He famously stated that he had never killed anyone unless his life had been in mortal danger. Bass waited until the storm abated before slinging the body of Dozier on his back and trekking back to the camp. Minewa, already back at the camp, had reported the tragedy of the likely death of Bass to the rest of the posse. When Flint showed up thirty minutes later without Bass, the worst was confirmed. The shackled cattle rustlers, silent in fear, wondered what fate awaited them with the death of Bass Reeves. All heads jerked up at the same moment at the sound of a loud whistle suddenly piercing the silence. Minewa hooted back and sprinted across the clearing to meet Bass. Minewa and the others hooted with jubilant astonishment and relief when Bass emerged from the woods edging the clearing, Dozier's body draped over his shoulder. Smoothing his mustache, he nodded to Minewa who understood the unspoken message… *That was a close call, that bullet came so close, it ruffled my mustache.*

On the long ride back to Fort Smith, Bass and his team nabbed two more outlaws who were accused of stealing guns and sheep from a Potawatomie family. Bass, always prepared to make arrests whenever the opportunity to cross the paths of an outlaw arrived, had no trouble finding the writs from the stack that Judge Parker provided him with before heading out to the Territories. Though Bass could not read, his remarkable memory assured him of never making a mistake in serving a warrant for an arrest. Bass attributed his never failing memory skills to the many years of card playing with the colonel when he was a young man.

Never one to waste time or effort on single manhunts, Judge Parker always supplied Bass with a thick wad of warrants ready to serve. Among them were writs for two Creeks charged with assault and rape, and multiple warrants for a gang of whiskey smugglers whom Bass suspected were staked out for the winter near Shawnee.

Of special interest to Bass was the ongoing investigation of the shocking homicide of a popular black circuit preacher, gunned down the previous autumn for igniting a fire that, fanned by a sudden wind, spread to his neighbor's ranch. Bass was given the challenging assignment to bring in Jim Webb, the much-wanted murderer who had fatally shot the preacher in the Chickasaw Nation. Webb believed the preacher had intentionally lost control of a grass fire that spread to the neighboring ranch where Webb was the foreman. Webb, a cruel and ruthless man, in charge of forty-five cowboys, most of whom were black, was known for his wild fury and preference to settle squabbles swiftly with his gun. When Webb confronted the sermonizer, who blamed the blaze on a sudden upsurge of unexpected wind, the angry argument inevitably escalated and abruptly terminated with a searing slug in the chest of the young preacher man who found himself at his beloved and much talked about Pearly Gates decades earlier than anticipated. The untimely death of the popular young minister stirred public opinion and debate about whether a posse should be recruited or lawmen brought in. It was decided that, when dealing with the unhinged Webb, it was more judicious to task the lawmen with the highly risky showdown.

Bass and his posse man, Sharpshoot, outlined their strategy. Webb's reputation as unpredictable and dangerous necessitated a well-thought-out plan since it was possible that Webb might shoot them both as they rode up to his ranch to serve the warrant. Always up to an occasion that would benefit from a cunning disguise to successfully apprehend an outlaw, Bass and Sharpshoot agreed to approach the ranch as any tenderfoot cowpoke partners in search of a hot meal or work would do. To further their plan, Bass and Sharpshoot laughed and spoke loudly, as if clearly unaware whose home they brazenly approached. Bass burst into a popular cattle trail song as they causally neared the ranch house. The large imposing log structure sported a wide, long front porch where three mangy dogs, roused from their siesta, barked and whined.

Webb and his cook greeted them with suspicious caution. Webb knew of Bass Reeves, as did most everyone in the Territories, and, as the two cowboys rode in laughing and talking, Webb observed with wariness the imposingly tall man wearing a kerchief on the lower half of his face, and his partner, who in Webb's opinion, was surely a foolish hayseed whose inane high-pitched laughter and cockeyed hat offered enough proof for Webb. As was customary, the two cowboys asked for a meal and a spot to water and rest their horses for a short time. They were short of funds and looking for work, they explained. They had heard of a successful rancher in the area who sometimes needed extra cowhands to manage his cattle.

Although Webb and his chef welcomed them, Bass noted Webb's two holstered pistols. Keenly aware that they were being scrutinized, Bass casually leaned his Winchester rifle against the front porch railing before leading Flint to the watering trough, a subtle gesture meant to convey trust and respect. Webb and the chef eyed Bass carefully before beckoning the two into a narrow room attached to the kitchen, where a large saucepan of chili and a pot of coffee bubbled on the wood stove. When the robust cook tossed a stained dishcloth over his broad shoulder after first mopping up the sweat from his forehead and wiping the damp cloth across the wood plank table, Bass suppressed a grimace. The chef carelessly slopped out generous servings of chili for the hungry men and set a loaf of bread in front of them and pulled up a chair to join in the meal. Webb kept a guarded eye on his guests as he chewed each spoonful laboriously, picking at his teeth between each bite with a long silver sewing needle. Sharpshoot and Bass enthusiastically slurped the spicy chili and tore off hunks of fresh bread from the shared loaf. Suddenly, for no apparent reason, Webb rose from the table and, with a slight tilt of his head, the chef bolted from his chair to follow him, a move that signaled to Bass that confrontation was imminent. A few moments later, they returned and, seating themselves at opposite corners of the table with hands on their pistols, Webb gave Bass a long hard stare. Still pretending to be a ranch hand, Bass launched into a long and rambling tale about a young rookie from the East who couldn't even saddle his own horse correctly. Sharpshoot laughed at the fictional memory and fabricated elaborate details. As they sought to amuse the unsmiling Webb and the chef with another far-flung story about a dimwitted lawman, one of the sickly hounds on the front porch barked, followed quickly by yelps from the two others. The second that Webb's head twisted towards the porch, Bass reached over the table, grabbed Webb in a choking grip with his left hand, and aimed his pistol with his right arm at the chef. *It is good to be ambidextrous,* thought Bass. Coughing and spluttering, Webb had no choice but to surrender. As the chef aimed his weapon to fire at Bass, Sharpshoot lurched towards him from the side, trying to knock the pistol out of his hand. The chef squeezed the trigger and sent a bullet that ricocheted off the iron stove with a screaming ping and just missing Bass by inches and lodging itself in the wall behind him. Trying to fire again, the chef struggled with Sharpshoot, who, with a swift maneuver, twisted the would-be killer to face Bass. With his free left hand, Bass shot the chef in his stomach without releasing his one-handed choke hold on Webb. Shooting the chef was not part of the plan, but both Bass and Sharpshoot were always quick to assess the danger of an unpredictable situation that offered no options. Bass and Sharpshoot handcuffed Webb and shackled him to the iron stove. In a humane attempt to staunch the seeping blood, Sharpshoot packed the wound with a jarful of honey and knotted the chili-stained cloth on the gaping wound. Double-checking that Webb could not escape, they lugged the fatally injured chef to a fence near their horses and then went back to pick up Webb. Tying the prisoners' legs with stout rope underneath the belly of the horses, Bass and Sharpshoot raced back to the campsite to load the two captives in a wagon before heading back to Fort Smith to turn them over to waiting marshals. The close-range gunshot suffered by the chef from Bass was too severe to withstand the arduous journey on the rough trail. Within two hours, his last breath gurgled out and the chef met his final reckoning. Though Bass did not have a warrant for the chef, he removed his boots and added them to the burlap bag of confiscated guns. Judge Parker might want them as evidence for the Webb case. The bulky body was unceremoniously abandoned in the Chickasaw lands in a small ravine bordering a grove of blackjacks. The teetering wagon clipped along and, as they headed off, Bass noted four black vultures dropping from the sky as they searched for the carrion tucked into the ravine.

Finally, the two horsemen and their prisoner reached their destination, Fort Smith, on the border of the Territories and Arkansas. Bass turned the hand-cuffed Webb over to federal agents for imprisonment and stashed the gold and silver dollars he was paid into a long beaded bag, secured to the inside of his vest. He smiled when he thought of Jennie and the clever secret pockets she sewed into all of his clothing. *It was a profitable venture*, thought Bass as he turned over the writ marked with his sign to the authorities. He felt great satisfaction at having both nabbed a dangerous criminal and earning a wad of cash and silver dollars to share with those he cared for. That Bass was known to hand out silver dollars to families, widows, or hard-working individuals, was a pleasure for Bass and the gratitude returned to him filled him with silent pride. So as to never embarrass the receivers of his gift, he would comment that he wanted to leave them with his calling card and hand them a silver dollar.

It was with great consternation that, shortly after less than a full year of imprisonment, Bass learned that Webb's accomplices and friends had met the sizeable $17,000 bail and Webb, unwisely, was released two months before his scheduled trial date. As Bass knew he would, Webb, supported by his network of outlaw friends and accomplices, vanished in a flash, back into the stateless lands. Bass was determined to apprehend Webb again and turn him over to Judge Parker, who, without doubt, would hang Webb on the famous Government Suspender.

For the next few months, Bass quietly listened to rumors and unfounded speculations about Webb's whereabouts. Some marshals thought Webb had headed for the Cherokee Strip, or perhaps he had high-tailed it to Old Mexico with his old friends and confederates, a safe destination for outlaws wanted in the states or territories since US lawmen would not track outlaws who made it that far south to cross the border. Old Mexico was a safe haven compared to any of the stateless territories north of its border. Bass suspected that Webb was too locked into the known lands to ride through the dangerous outreaches beyond. Webb would never survive life alone in Old Mexico.

Months later, a reliable source, his old friend, Tuska-homa, confided to Bass that Webb had recently been seen more than once at the Chickasaw Nation trading post. Bass also heard from his barber that a man, who met the description of Webb but called himself Jeb, had recently needed three teeth pulled. Under the watch of two partners, ready at the gun, the barber poured Jeb a large cup of whiskey to gulp down before taking his sturdy little plyers in hand and extracting two rotten molars and one front tooth in three swift yanks. Bass remembered Webb's slow chewing and the silver needle he used to pick his teeth. He never believed that Webb had left the territories, despite the many rumors that were floated. Webb was not the sort of outlaw, like Dozier, to operate alone and he needed his powerful network of associates, other evil-doers who had raised his bond money and freed him from the clutches of Judge Parker and a trial at the Court of the Damned. Bass wondered how many hidden caches of money had been discovered and robbed to have come up with the high bond.

Bass, Tuska-homa, and Minewa's brother, Dancing Horse, immediately planned a raid to capture Webb while he had still been sighted in the area. He was unflinchingly steadfast in his determination to bring Webb into custody again. Not only had he succeeded in capturing the highly dangerous Webb less than a year before, but he had to kill a man in self-defense. That Webb had managed to evade justice and possibly the Government Suspender was a personal issue for Bass. After the hard work to nab him and the inadvertent shooting in self-defense of Webb's cook, his release and subsequent escape did not settle well.

Wanting to assure minimal suspicion, Bass thought carefully about the camouflage he would use this time to carry out the risky charade he carefully planned. He substituted his usual black hat with a worn, wide-brimmed sombrero, combed his bushy mustache over his upper lip, and selected a large handwoven serape given to him by Jennie to conceal his hidden weapons. A faded blue bandanna wrapped around the bottom half of his face completed his outfit. He slipped his small Derringer into his boot and pocketed the two six-shooters in preparation for the encounter. Not wanting to be seen together with his partner, Bass shadowed Tuska-homa and Dancing Horse, who rode ahead, and, after blocking the back exit of the trade store with a length of wood, Tuska-homa casually sauntered in with a plan to chat up the clientele and the talkative manager, Cyrus Nightingale, to gather more information. In an unexpected stroke of fortune, Webb, now beardless and heavier, was there… loudly arguing with an itinerant fur trader. Claiming the prices were extravagantly high, he raised his voice and swore that he would never pay one more silver dollar for the stack of beaver pelts the trader displayed. Tuska-homa, with a barely perceptible gesture, signaled Bass who waited outside chatting amiably with an old cowboy leading his tired horse to the communal watering trough. With a tip of his hat to the old wrangler and humming one of his favorite melodies, Bass walked slowly to the store and swung open the Dutch doors. As he ambled in, he tossed one flap of the serape over a shoulder and nodded to the young boy sweeping the dusty plank floor. The boy looked up and Bass pointed a thumb towards the exit warning him to get out. The thirteen-year-old child, already well-versed in the language of hand gestures and eye blinks, dropped the broom and slipped outside, scooting to the back of the shop. He immediately noticed that the backdoor to the store was blocked and prudently took cover in a tool shed adjacent to the door to wait for the sound of gunshots.

Webb, in a loud voice, persisted to argue with the silver haired trapper, now irritated and packing up his pelts and skins, ready to head to the next trading post.

Bass glided slowly toward the counter, weaving through the store aisles of pickles, sauerkraut, and jams, his hands lightly fondling both of his six-shooters. Intuition or perhaps it was suspicion born of experience, sparked in Webb's chest as he wheeled around to face the strangely familiar-looking old Mexican drover edging closer. *It's Reeves, that damn lawman up to his tricks again*! Webb grabbed both his Winchester rifle and his revolver from the counter and lunged toward the unexpectedly blocked back door. Careening around barrels of nails grouped on the floor in the rear of the shop, Webb circled around and vaulted like an antelope through the front door, and, with a wild whoop, leaped on his horse, spurs digging into the ribcage of the speckled Appaloosa he rode. Galloping full speed into a scruffy thicket of trees, he twisted his body and fired towards Bass who was hot on his trail. Webb's bullet zinged through Bass's hat brim and the second bullet split the leather reins Bass grasped. Still, he was no match for the crackerjack marksman, Bass Reeves, and, with one straight shot, Bass downed him. Tumbling off his panicked horse, he landed on his back with his right hand resting on his bloody chest. As he lay dying, a crowd formed as if out of nowhere and joined the customers who had been sheltering behind the store. They gathered around to watch the final scene play out. They were not disappointed as they watched the tall man who had shot Webb come close. Flinging off the serape, Bass walked toward the dying man. The silver star pinned to his vest flashed in the bright sunlight and a respectful hush fell over the onlookers as they stared at the fearless and renowned lawman approaching ever nearer to the still-breathing Webb.

Webb limply tossed his revolver to the side and gestured weakly to Bass. With no fear, Bass crouched down and, to the surprise of all, Webb offered his slack hand to congratulate Bass and bequeathed him his revolver with a nod as a gift of admiration of Bass's prowess and determination in nabbing him. With a few last gasps, Webb died. When Bass was later interviewed about this, he was equally admiring in his praise for Webb and described him as the bravest and meanest man with whom he had ever wrangled. The close call and the shootout that ended in Bass's favor, followed by Webb turning over his weapon as a gift was a scene that was branded in Bass's mind forever, and also to those who witnessed the dramatic demise of Webb.

Bass treasured the old hat that Webb had shot a hole through. Not only was the hat a dramatic reminder of fallibility and an entertaining prop that embellished his stirring and suspenseful storytelling, but it was also, in Bass's mind, evidence of the unseen forces that never failed him when he needed protection. The clever disguises, cagey tricks, winning charm, reputation for fairness, and expert marksmanship conspired together to form a protective shield around Bass. Never seriously injured or maimed, Bass attributed his good fortune, in part, to the pouches of mysterious items given to him by his old friend, Chief Two Moons, and the long-ago gifts of Chief of the Muskogee.

Bass and Tuska-homa headed back to the concealed camp where twelve miserable prisoners had been shackled together under guard for two days and began the arduous journey back to Fort Smith to deliver the captives to Judge Parker. They swaddled Webb in the serape that Bass had used as part of his artful disguise. The convicts were of diverse ethnicity; Bass could never be accused of bias or fear when encountering any miscreant. The prisoners mirrored the population of the Indian Territories: white, black, Mexican, and Native Americans of any tribe could be nabbed and brought to Judge Parker. Their crimes were equally diverse… whiskey smuggling, horse and cattle theft, arson, rape, stagecoach robbery, homicide, and property swindling. Since officers of the law had the right to arrest someone on the spot committing a crime, Bass could appraise any suspect situation and assert his authority when necessary. Such was the case when he headed back to Fort Smith after another hard and dangerous manhunt.

Riding through a dry creek bed edged by thick stands of cane, Bass heard angry shouts. Urging Flint to gallop faster, Bass scattered gravel and rock-hard clods of the parched earth as he careened around a bend and saw a solitary tree on the banks of the Arkansas River. It was obvious to Bass that the two men he saw were preparing to lynch a youth who was strapped in an unnatural position to the wide trunk. Bass watched closely as one of the men untied the victim and tried to hoist the struggling young boy, hands roped behind his back, on a horse. The agitated horse, whose sudden bolt when smacked hard on the haunch would break the man's neck, was uncooperative and the killer's accomplice held the reins tight as the other floundered with the awkward task of lifting the tethered boy. A heavy hemp noose already dangled from a limb. Before they could loop the rope around the victim's neck, Bass fired off his two Colt. 45s and blasted toward the men. At the sight of a lawman wearing a star-shaped badge, the killers split in different directions, each in a mad scramble for the hills beyond. Bass dismounted, cut the rough rope from the boy's hands, and freed the young man. A long drink from Bass's canteen revived the terrified boy, *only a child*, Bass thought, as he lifted the weakened adolescent to the front of the saddle and mounted Flint, to ride back to the sheltered haven of a nearby Cherokee village where his family lived. Forever indebted to Bass, the youthful Cherokee brave Bass had rescued later proved to be a helpful informant when needed. His gratitude to Bass was paid back in the many tips he shared. The young boy did not know the assailants who had ambushed him at the river and tried to kill him, or why, and attributed the attempted crime to vile racism that randomly reared its ugly head against successful blacks or Indians. The family confirmed that a couple of rough-looking strangers had been shadowing the small settlement for several days looking for trouble. They had followed one of the women on the trail to the river bank but streaked off when her brother rode up to join her. Bass promised he would report the incident to the Lighthorse Mounted Police and keep his eyes and ears open for any information about their whereabouts.

Badly in need of a rest and a visit home, Bass met up with his posse a few miles east of the unexpected encounter and headed back to Arkansas with the newest menagerie of desperados. One severely wounded outlaw died on the rugged journey. Bass took his battered shabby boots as evidence of his capture and left the body propped up in a grove of trees, a warning recognized by all shady characters that Bass was in the area and not to be trifled with. The eight other prisoners hunkered down in the wagon, morosely reflecting on their reckless deeds as they promised an unseen god that the straight and narrow would be their future path, should they be given another chance, possible… but… unlikely with Hanging Judge Parker. Judge Parker, all knew, had indeed pardoned a few criminals brought to him, usually a charitable decision influenced by the young age of a convict carted in from The Territories. The captives were distracted from their glum thoughts and the long and uncomfortable journey when Bass began singing *The Lament of the Cowboy*, a favored ballad with some mournful lyrics that no doubt resonated with the convicts.

There was always a warm and jubilant welcoming for Bass when he and his posse rode into town. Bass and his men never returned to Fort Smith without a crowd gathering around, as they hauled in the desperadoes, thieves, and wanted outlaws from the stateless lands. Judge Parker and his number one deputy were committed to corralling all criminals who tried to escape from the law by burrowing deep into the untamed wild lands. Not all of the accused captives managed to survive the strenuous trip back to Arkansas, and many of the wounded dodged certain hanging and perished en route. With every death en route, Bass offered a short prayer for their salvation. Like his boss, Judge Parker, who had never once witnessed an execution his judgment had delivered, but instead prayed for the souls of the sentenced, Bass too believed that even the worst deserved at least a passing flash of respect.

Narrow escapes from death were routine. Outlaws, often traveling in gangs, worked together to evade capture. Bass is said to have only killed fourteen men during his long career, but he brought three thousand accused criminals to the court during his three decades of serving as a lawman. Although Bass was greatly feared by the desperadoes and outlaws, he was lionized by those whose lives he had saved or had succeeded in returning the stolen horses, cattle, cash, or weapons to the rightful owners. His successful captures of criminals were much praised and celebrated by the unhappy victims of the thieving or murdering miscreants. Each of his three decades of successful work routing out the felons, murderers, rustlers, and connivers brought Bass more fame and respect and added to Bass's legendary reputation as an honest and just law officer.

One of the few men that Bass killed was Tom Story, leader of a horse-thieving gang operating in the Territories. For five long years, Story and his cohorts stole mules and horses, moving them in midnight runs to Texas, just across from their cleverly concealed hideout near the Red River that formed the border between the Territories and the state of Texas. Bass was, of course, very familiar with the area. He knew every path and well-worn trail that laced through the scruffy land and assured Judge Parker that he would arrest Tom Story and haul him back to the court.

In addition to the profitable horse theft business, Story seldom made the run back to the territories without a few kegs of moonshine which would always guarantee him extra profit. Bass, on temporary assignment in Paris, Texas, went after Story when the gang reversed their routine and stole a herd of valuable horses from a wealthy Texan rancher to sell in the old Indian Nation. The many possible hideaways and trails on the northern side of the Red River were well known to Bass and, within a couple of days, Bass discovered Story's cleverly camouflaged camp behind a thick stand of cane. Waiting patiently for Story to return, Bass positioned himself in readiness for the inevitable encounter. Within an hour, Bass heard the rhythmic clip of hooves on the rocky shale trotting toward the camp. Oblivious to the presence of danger, Story dismounted his stallion and stood still for a few moments listening to the breeze rattle the long fronds of cane. He heaved a loud sigh and, convinced he was safe and that no one had followed him, he put down his rifle and strode toward a small stack of wood to prepare for his evening meal. This was the moment Bass was waiting for and, in a thundering voice, he confronted the spooked man with the writ. As Story dropped the wood and grabbed for his six-shooter in a futile attempt to bring down the uninvited guest, Bass, as always, was quicker on the draw and that was the end of Tom's story.

Once, ambushed in a ravine by three dim-witted brothers for whom he had warrants, Bass persuaded them that he would have to record information about his own demise on the warrant after turning over his rifle to them. He innocently asked for the date and location of his capture. Unaware that Bass could neither write nor read, the illiterate brothers gleefully allowed him this last liberty. Before Bass turned his back to his would-be killers, he tapped the concealed bag of magic herbs as if to conjure up its protective power. Leaning the writ against his saddlebag, Bass gave the bushwhackers a moment to chuckle quietly at the famed lawman whose imminent departure from this world would reward the luckless brothers the fame and respect they yearned for and certainly deserved. Their mistaken calculation of the situation doomed them before they could congratulate each other. In one blazing moment, Bass swirled around and fired his two concealed pistols with both hands, dispatching the two brothers to the Great Beyond. The third brother cowered on the ground, his hands covering his head and trembling in fear. Bass whipped out his ever-ready cuffs, served the writ, and marched him back to the camp to join another six outlaws under the protective eyes of his loyal posse, Tuska-homa, Minewa, Sharpshoot, and Otis. Otis and Tuska-homa returned to the site and hoisted the two dead men onto the 'transport pony" to carry them back to the weather-beaten wagon. After removing their boots, the two men were placed upright and tied back to back against the trunk of a cottonwood tree. The small cross they etched into the bark of the tree was a gesture of courtesy and frontier custom, having nothing to do, in this case, with respect for the deceased. *God would take care of what they could not*, as Judge Parker often said.

As they journeyed back to Arkansas, Bass and his posse reminisced about one of their more dramatic and successful ruses. A Wells Fargo stagecoach loaded with gold and silver coins was hijacked en route from St. Louis, Missouri, on the Overland Trail passing through Kansas. The three armed bandits held up the coach at a safe distance from any nearby town in a long prepared assault that had originated with a fourth partner carefully monitoring the scheduled pick up from the main bank in St. Louis. The infamous and ruthless McFlynn gang specialized in coach holdups, always managing to elude capture by fleeing to the Indian Territories to stash their plundered bounty in one of the many well-concealed caves that riddled the San Bois Mountains. After depositing the loot and unencumbered by their heavy load, the gang routinely hid out for weeks or even months before returning to recover and divvy up their stolen booty. One member of the McFlynn gang always remained camped out near the hidden treasure in case it was necessary to dispatch some bumbler who heedlessly wandered too close for comfort.

Next to the stout stagecoach driver stood the armed guard, sharp-eyed and ears peeled for any sign of trouble. As he twisted and turned to survey the surroundings from his perch, he hoisted the double-barreled shotgun from one shoulder to the other, ready to fire in any direction. The McFlynn gang split up, with two of the highway robbers charging ahead. Danny Jay, the youngest member of the gang, tucked his lanky body into a shallow gully a few feet from the trail and listened for the approaching sound of pounding hooves, rifle at the ready. When the horse-drawn coach rounded the nearby small bend, Danny fired his rifle in the general direction of the stagecoach, causing the four horses to rear up in a sudden panic. The guard swirled around to fire back, but Danny had already slithered down into the rut and fired again, this time, bringing down one of the horses. The three other horses fell in the tangle of leads and reins, and the swaying coach came to an abrupt stop. This was the moment the other three McFlynn boys were waiting for and, in a mad rush from the overlooking small bluff, they surrounded the coach. The driver and the guard threw down their weapons at the command of the masked men and tumbled the heavy box of treasure over the side of the coach. Heaving the heavy load on one of the horses, the gang yelled victory cheers as they raced south.

Within a couple of hours, the McFlynn brothers crossed the border and were safe in the Territories with the loot. With no fear of state or federal law, the gang headed further south to the mountainous and rocky area they knew was honeycombed with caves.

Danny Jay, the youngest and cockiest member of the gang, not yet humbled by life or experience, could not resist gleefully crowing about his significant role in the successful heist once they arrived in the Cherokee Nation. Still far to go, and not yet as safe as he imagined, he blustered with self-importance, bragging to anyone who would listen that he had been assigned as the advance guard and had severely injured one of the horses of the team that pulled the coach... no small role when holding up an armed coach... and especially a Wells Fargo coach transporting more than a hundred and fifty pounds of treasure in the strongbox beneath the driver's seat. Knowing they were not being chased, the gang let their guard down, spending each night in a different village and indulging in what minimal entertainment was available. Danny Jay's loose tongue and boisterous behavior quickly became a subject of gossip and reached the ear of one of the Lighthorse Police assigned to the region. Quickly and unexpectedly, Danny Jay was arrested and charged with unseemly and drunk behavior and hauled into the jail in Fort Smith. His comrades scattered and met at the designated trail that twisted deep into the San Bois Mountains. Undismayed and confident that the court had no basis on which to hold him, Danny Jay continued to boast proudly about the thrill of the successful holdup to another inmate. *Hmmm... juicy information, reward-worthy info, no doubt*, the listener considered, prying for greater detail from the young braggart who did not hesitate to share the full scheme of the successful takedown of the Well Fargo coach. Aiming for reward money or leniency, the inmate naturally and immediately shared the scoop with one of the surly, but inquisitive jailhouse guards. The tip was duly reported the next day and the snitch's sentence was promised to be reduced should the information prove accurate.

Wells Fargo management was fully determined to retrieve the stolen haul of highly valued notes, gold, and silver and discussed how they could entrap the thieves. Their plan was a simple con that had been successful before. They would, with the approval of Judge Parker, plant an informant in the jail. Bass's sidekick, Minewa, was selected to go undercover on a trumped-up charge to convince Danny Jay that he would be able to spring him... in exchange for a mere quarter of his cut of the hidden stash. Minewa, arrested for cattle rustling and bootlegging, was brought to the court by Bass, where he was escorted to the jail pending trial. In the nefarious and filthy jail, crowded with miscreants from every corner of the Territories, Minewa befriended Danny Jay and the two of them commiserated about the corrupt law officers who had locked them up without evidence or a trial. Minewa assured Danny Jay that escape was possible and explained that, fortunately, one of the night guards owed him a sizable favor and, if Danny Jay agreed to repay Minewa with a generous share of his stake in the treasure, he would set the gears in action for a midnight escape. Danny eagerly agreed, knowing that his brothers would help him deal with Minewa once they made it safely to the western side of Hell's Fringe. The dark cover of night shielded the guard's face and Danny paid little attention to the unusually tall, silent man who unlocked the cell, slipped a weapon to Minewa, and led both escapees to one saddled horse to make their run, an obvious precaution that would deter Danny from making a lone run.

All went as planned. Followed by Bass and two other deputies, Danny Jay rode directly to the camp near the well-concealed hideout and breathlessly told the story to the McFlynn brothers who were awakened in the dead of night by the rhythmic beat of pounding hooves. To give Minewa time to ferret out the exact spot where the cash was stashed, Bass and the two deputies, unruffled, waited in the darkness at a discrete distance. When he heard the agreed-upon signal—the long hooting of a barn owl— Bass and his men swooped down the small canyon and arrested the gang. Surrounded by four heavily armed men, the McFlynns surrendered without a shot being fired. With the shackles in place, the posse loaded up the treasure in capacious bags brought for that purpose and headed back to Arkansas with the four felons. A Wells Fargo detective smiled at the criminals as he greeted the lawmen and their captives on arrival at the courthouse. It was a successful raid that both Minewa and Bass enjoyed retelling to captive listeners and they eagerly embellished each account.

Chapter 12

Losses and Transition

As the century drew to an end, the population of white settlers had increased threefold from sixty thousand to two hundred thousand in a mere fifteen years. With increasing boldness and ever-growing greed, the federal government eyed the Territories, No Man's Land, and two million acres in the middle of the vast area, the Unassigned Lands, which had not been designated for use by any one tribe. In 1879, as more and more settlers pressured Congress and the courts to open the Unassigned Lands, President Hays, stood in support of past treaties with the tribes, forbidding Europeans to settle in the land already promised to the Indians. Anger, frustration, and avarice drove many settlers to join up with the incendiary firebrand, David Payne, from Kansas, who was unstoppable in his push for the settlement and development of the Territories. David Payne and his followers, who wanted to establish a white colony, snuck into the reserved lands three times and, three times, they were arrested and escorted out. Judge Parker, friend to the tribes, had ruled against Payne in the past but allowed him to return to Kansas, where Payne continued to rile up the farmers and businessmen in Kansas.

In 1889, after the first land run, a federal court tasked with dealing with the non-Indian population was established in the newly settled land, reducing Judge Parker's jurisdiction. Appeals to the Supreme Court were now allowed for the newly established federal court, further diminishing Judge Parker's reach. The reduced jurisdiction did not, however, lessen the heavy workload of Judge Parker's court or his lawmen. The increasing flow of settlers and opportunists brought more conflict and kept the court busy six days a week, with the quarter terms running into each other without break. Law-abiding settlers had to contend with the many fugitives from justice from surrounding states who had joined the land runs. The Twin Territories swarmed with renegade outlaws who rendezvoused with old partners in the chaotic times. Other gangs hid out in the northeastern towns of Indian Territory and acted as fences for the cattle rustlers and horse thieves out west. The lawmen from Judge Parker's court remained diligent in their mission to routing out as many thieves, rapists, and murderers as they could capture.

In 1890, the western portion of the Indian Territories became incorporated and was now known as the Oklahoma Territories. Life in the old Indian Nation was undergoing massive transformations and was now split into the Oklahoma Territory and the Indian Territory, better known as the Twin Territories. Chaos continued to reign with even greater numbers of outlaws taking advantage of the stateless status of the Twin Territories.

The Court of the Western District of Arkansas under Judge Isaac Parker's tenure had dealt out justice for more than twenty years in the country's most dangerous and lawless land but, by 1896, most of the worst of the desperados had been arrested and jailed. Word had spread that the Territories were no longer a safe haven for criminals, as it was soon to become a new state of the union, bound by both federal and state laws. Development of towns, roads, railroads, and business boomed, and the presence of the law was everywhere. The Cherokee Strip and the western part of the Oklahoma Territory were open to settlement, a sure sign that statehood loomed on the horizon. It was unimaginable to many tribal leaders that, once again, the treaties and past agreements were being betrayed, and fevered talk that perhaps two states might be created—Oklahoma and Sequoyah, fed false hope to the tribes.

Judge Isaac Parker was scheduled to serve at the opening of the new federal court in Arkansas the following month but, for the first time in his career, Judge Parker was incapacitated and unable to fulfill his duties. Two months later, he died from Bright's disease, a fatal kidney malfunction. A couple of months later, Jennie died from an undetermined illness. The death of both Judge Parker and his wife, the two most significant people in his life within a few months of each other, was a hard blow for Bass. There were no words of comfort from friends that could fill the emptiness or diminish his anguish. Stunned and saddened, Bass's emotions churned as he tried to come to peace with the loss of his beloved wife, Jennie, and the man, whose early trust and confidence in Bass Reeves, an African-American slave freed by the Emancipation Acts, had propelled his much-loved career as a lawman.

Though the Honorable Judge Isaac Parker remained a controversial figure throughout much of his life and after his death, his fierce dedication to the rule of law earned him fame and respect among both friends and enemies. His funeral was attended by thousands. While the condemned convicts in jail cheered and journalists in the East wrote lengthy diatribes questioning the morality of the judge, the tribes of the Indian Nation and the law-abiding communities bordering the dangerous haven for ruthless murderers mourned the loss of their staunchest supporter. During his twenty-three year tenure as federal judge, he heard more than thirteen thousand four hundred cases. Of the one hundred and sixty Judge Parker condemned to the gallows, eighty sentences were commuted or retried. Seventy-nine people were executed, while the other condemned men were pardoned, died in prison, or their sentences were commuted to life imprisonment instead of capital punishment.

Judge Rogers was appointed by President Cleveland as the successor to Judge Parker. Bass was transferred to Muskogee and worked for Marshal Bennet as the marshal's right hand and most trusted deputy. Bass continued the dangerous work of routing out outlaws, accepting every dangerous assignment given to him. Bass was grateful that his friends and marshals continued to work for the new judge.

Bass remarried a few years after Jennie's untimely death from illness. When Bass met Abigail, a widow with a child, he knew that Jennie would welcome a second marriage. Abigail accepted Bass's proposal and, with little fanfare, they married. Comforting and kind, Abigail had an instinctive understanding of Bass's need for respite from his dangerous days hunting down outlaws and the desperadoes who still sought refuge in the Territories. Abigail, like Jennie, enjoyed having home parties, and old friends and new guests continued to visit Bass.

As usual, Bass entertained the guests with wild tales about his arrests and adventures. When asked about female lawbreakers, Bass liked to talk about Belle Starr, the famed female outlaw, known to all as the "Bandit Queen" and to whom he had to serve a writ for horse theft. Belle willingly accompanied Bass to Fort Smith, not wanting to risk tarnishing her reputation by arriving in handcuffs. Bass waited patiently out on the front porch as she decked herself out and spent too long selecting the proper outfit and hat for her entrance into the court. Despite Belle's dubious reputation and alliances with numerous shady men and wanted outlaws, Bass and Belle maintained a friendship that was of mutual benefit. He would at times warn her of violent outlaws sighted in the area, and she would pass on confidential information about the lying and thieving miscreants who had wronged her and did not deserve her discretion or protection.

Bass reminded his guests that Belle Starr was also helpful in his arrest of Pastor Goodwin. Several months before Judge Rogers had suggested that Bass take on the unpleasant assignment, but not dangerous, to serve a warrant to Pastor Isaac Goodwin, a local Baptist preacher and a friend of Belle Starr. Arresting any man of the cloth was unsettling for Bass but, after nearly three decades of working the Territories, he knew that many a charlatan hid devious motives behind the guise of a preacher man. It was a well-kept secret among a few of the churchgoers that the pastor was engaged in some shady business deals in the Cherokee Nation having to do with smuggling and selling illegal alcohol. Lydia Howerton and Gertie Gottlieb, wives of two of Pastor Goodwin's customers, confided to each other that both their husbands enjoyed a tumbler or two of beer or whiskey every evening. Somehow, there seemed to be a free-flowing supply and neither man ever ran low. The word was out among some of the male parishioners. The number of guests dropping by the Gottlieb and Howerton homes increased steadily, interrupting the quiet evenings Lydia and Gertie had previously enjoyed with the family. The children too were being deprived of the company and instruction of their fathers. The women commiserated, concurring with each other that the situation was untenable and that it was their Christian duty to remedy the crisis. Both suspected the pastor of corruption. They agreed that Pastor Goodwin must be the culprit supplying the illegal alcohol. Gertie initiated the conversation with her often repeated aphorism; *God's mill grinds slowly, but surely.*

Lydia adjusted her bonnet strings, lowered her head, and nodded. Together, they conspired to get rid of the trouble-causing preacher who was debasing and corrupting their husbands by peddling the Devil's brew. After much discussion, with Gertie taking the lead, it was decided that Lydia's role would be to alert the Indian Lighthorse Police, who, in turn, would pass the information on to the federal marshals. This strategy would assure anonymity for them, for they did not want the church community to be privy to their domestic affairs. Gertie was adamant about that. Another consideration was that both women were aware that some members of the church held a high regard for Pastor Goodwin, and their potential fury at having the pastor ousted might encourage the misguided to pass on a warning, allowing the pastor to make a clean break and avoid justice.

It was Belle Starr who persuaded Bass to allow the pastor to give his last Sunday sermon in peace so as not to subject the bootlegger to unnecessary embarrassment in front of his mostly law-abiding and devoted flock. Those in the community who did not suspect the pastor of harboring any worldly desires would learn soon enough about the pastor's side job, Belle sympathized. It was clear to Bass that Pastor Goodwin was not a stranger to Belle and the two of them shared undisclosed business interests. Not wanting to speculate further on the relationship between Belle and the pastor, he did not question her and took her advice.

On Sunday morning, he secured Flint to the tall chinaberry tree near the dirt path that led to the church. Bass hoped that the pastor would surrender peacefully when he served the warrant. Biding his time outside the small cabin that served as a church, Bass wondered how Isaac Goodwyn had strayed so far. Listening from outside, Bass could hear the booming voice of the pastor exhorting his followers to cleave to the path of virtue and shun evil in all its varied forms. Bass was not judgmental of nonviolent offenses, but he was philosophical and thoughtful. It was not the first time he wondered about errant behavior that conflicted with the values of a chosen profession. The hymn the congregation sang roused a childhood memory of life back in Texas when he was a slave, so many years ago. Bass allowed himself a moment of nostalgia and closed his eyes to listen. Slowly, the congregation drifted out and gathered in small groups visiting together and sharing news. Bass dismounted and waited patiently for the small community of churchgoers to head back to their homes to enjoy the rest of the pleasant Sunday afternoon with their families. When the last couple had rounded the corner and he could no longer hear the clip clapping of horse hooves or laughing children on the path, Bass entered the church and served the warrant to the startled pastor who was seated on one of the planks that served as the pew and carefully counting the meager coins in the donation basket. A wrapped packet of cheese, a small basket of berries, and a few eggs were evidently included in the parishioners' charitable contributions.

Pastor Goodwin did not resist arrest and, after securing the church and packing his Bible in his saddlebag, Bass and Pastor Goodwin headed back to Arkansas. Bass followed a short distance behind in case the distraught and sweating preacher decided to bolt. Though the pastor did consider the option, he judiciously weighed the risk and hoped for Judge Roger's leniency. Perhaps, he hoped, the judge and his shared devoutness to scripture might be of benefit. On the other hand, the Honorable Judge might be compelled to point out his evident weakness and laxity in not being able to abide by the words of the sacred text.

The pastor shifted uncomfortably in his saddle and sweat beaded on his forehead when he heard Bass humming the familiar melody of Amazing Grace. Even though Bass was not singing, every word of the old hymn thrummed through the pastor. Pastor Goodwin struggled with his personal demons as he unsuccessfully searched for any justification for his deeds. He confided to Bass that it was a tightly snarled knot he could not unravel. *Would sufficiently displayed remorse credit him with a lesser fine and sentence?* he wondered out loud. Bass did not answer.

Bass concluded the story by assuring the guests that the pastor, having not committed a violent crime or a theft, was charged with the illegal sale of alcohol and given a weighty fine. Judge Rogers decided he should serve time in the notorious jail, known by all as Hell on the Border, where he could make amends by ministering to the prisoners. When Pastor Goodwin was released four weeks later, he quickly relocated to Texas where he prayed he could resume his ministry in one of the many small towns far south where no one would know of his past deeds. As he traveled south to cross the Red River, the pastor contemplated the abrupt change of direction his life had taken in the preceding four weeks. Despite the promises he made and sermons he had delivered to fellow inmates when incarcerated, the pastor became increasingly aware of his parched throat and an urgent thirst that could only be relieved in one way. With a few quick smacks of his riding crop on the hind quarter of his horse, he sped on towards the border of the Indian Nation.

Chapter 13

A Heartbreaking Manhunt

By the turn of the century, much had changed in the Oklahoma and Indian Territories and there was exuberant talk of statehood. Bass was diligent in continuing his work to arrest criminals, bringing in ox carts crowded with convicts shackled together. In one momentous swoop, Bass brought in a diverse group of twenty-four miserable men, but not before giving all of them his famed lectures on morality and the law. The mounted police of the tribal nations, known as the Lighthorse Police, worked side by side with the lawmen as they tried to maintain order and justice for the victims of ongoing theft, plunder, murder, or rape. The Lighthorse men were fully authorized to charge and arrest members of tribal communities but, if the crime had been committed by a non-Indian, then the accused would be turned over to the judge's posse men or lawmen.

Bass counted on the confidence, loyalty, linguistic expertise, and physical help given to him by the Lighthorse Police. He admired their dedication to duty despite the betrayals they had suffered from the federal government. Bass knew that most, or all, of the land promised to the tribes would be taken, and that it was only a matter of time before the Territories would be granted statehood as powerful men conspired and schemed to control the development and prosperity of the Territories.

Unknown to Bass, the most difficult days lay ahead, more challenging even than the nearly successful ambush by the three horse-thieving, murdering brothers. Bass reached Fort Smith and turned in the writs to Judge Rogers, collected his salary and the bounty pay, and headed home to spend a couple of weeks with his family and town friends. He imagined enjoyable evenings, good meals, and the company of Abigail and the children. Most of all, he anticipated a short time in which vigilance was not required, and a week or two of relaxation with his family and friends would revitalize him. Family time, hot baths, dinner guests, and time to catch up with neighbors and friends served as restorative medicine for Bass. As always, when Bass showed up, his family was ecstatic and prepared a grand welcoming feast for the next day, inviting old and new friends to share the family's celebration. Bass had been gone from home for a few weeks and there was always the unspoken fear that one day he would not return.

After a deep sleep in a comfortable and welcoming bed, Bass woke early, as was his habit, and settled in for a tranquil day of checking his property, indulging his and Abigail's children, and preparing for the festive home party later in the afternoon. He polished his boots, cleaned his weapons, and checked on his horses, happily nosing around in the pasture munching on the sweet grass. He chopped a load of oak and cedar to be used later in the evening and took a walk around the pasture accompanied by his beloved dogs. The young family members helped prepare for the evening by stacking the wood near the outdoor cooking area. Bass was sorry to see that his eldest son, Ben, who sometimes served with Marshal Hart's posse, was not there.

The late afternoon pot-luck picnic was well attended and Bass's off duty colleagues joined the gathering. The lavish trays and platters of food provided by guests displayed the usual impressive array of roasted meats, potato salads, pecan and apple pies, beans, and large platters of fresh fried catfish, bass, and bluegill hooked only hours before from the Arkansas River. The outdoor stone oven was heaped with baking breads, and chicken and beef sizzled on the grill while several young people took turns stoking the fire.

The convivial camaraderie that permeated the cheerful gathering was welcomed by Bass. It was a time to exchange news and share updates about family and friends. Many people lingered well into the evening. He hoped his son, Ben, was safe and commented to one of the visiting lawmen that he wondered who Marshal Hart and Ben were planning to surprise that night. The apparently distracted guest turned away and, instead of answering Bass, he grabbed one of the rambunctious children who ran through the household and lifted the squealing boy high above his shoulders. The thought crossed Bass's mind that he would ask later about Ben and his mission later in the evening when the excitement of the party wore down. There was too much commotion, and it was not the right time to talk about work.

Finally, late in the evening, the party began to wind down. Two friends played fiddles and banjos while two couples of young people with shy smiles danced together, an acceptable and thrilling foreplay to a possible courtship. The musicians packed up their fiddles and the couple split off to return home with their weary parents. Slowly, the remaining families and lone stragglers drifted off into the night, and the crowd thinned out. With the last guests departed, Abigail bid the men goodnight and went to bed. The children, worn out from chasing and tumbling with each other, fell asleep on the quilted pallets lined up in a room in the back of the house. Two of the children's friends had fallen asleep hours before, cuddled up on the old and worn buffalo rug that had been given to Bass so long ago when he married Jennie. The house became quiet and the few remaining male guests settled in front of the still-glowing light of the fireplace and the flickering candles. Strange shadows danced and rippled across the room and Bass and his old friends sat in comfortable silence together.

The few men who had stayed to smoke and drink gradually clustered around Bass who welcomed their safe friendship. His old friend and posse man, Sharpshoot, skinny as ever, gave Bass a tight bear hug. Three lawmen and one prosecutor Bass knew well joined them. They fondly reminisced and exchanged stories about Judge

Parker and wondered what he would have thought about the rumors of statehood for Oklahoma and the Indian Territories. Bass and his friends agreed that the best solution favored by the tribes was the optional plan for the creation of two states. A compromise and a resolution that should satisfy all, they agreed, would be the creation of two states: Oklahoma in the west for the settlers, and Sequoyah for the Indian Nation. They underestimated the hunger of the powerful industrialists, the oil barons, and the land-seeking settlers.

As the lively conversation died down, Bass sensed a shift in the mood among the guests. Lengthy pauses and downcast eyes alerted Bass that the five men were stalling but had something of great urgency to spill. It was the worst news that Bass could have imagined. His own son, Ben, had been charged with a violent murder two days before. Bass was stunned. The sympathetic friends reluctantly detailed the crime that Ben was accused of. Not only was Ben now a wanted killer and a fugitive, but Bass had the double shock of hearing that Ben had killed his wife, Lucile, in a blast of jealous rage when he walked into his home unexpectedly and found his wife in a feverish embrace with another man.

As a posse man, Ben was gone for long stretches of time, leaving Lucile lonely and isolated on their small farm near Muskogee. She was an easy mark for the green-eyed transient charmer who stopped to rest and catch up on any news in the area. Seduced by his soothing voice and polite manner, Lucile resisted little when he reached for her. Ben and Lucile suffered through this first betrayal by acknowledging mutual blame and, with renewed commitment, they stayed together.

In the months that followed, Ben turned down work that would take him far from home for days or even a week at a time. He was more attentive to Lucile and peace reigned in their small household again. Lucile and Ben talked often about their future. *Maybe it was time to have a child*, Lucile suggested. Feeling that the relationship was now more stabilized, they decided that the cash brought in by occasional posse work would be welcomed, even if it meant a few days of absence. Ben alerted the marshal that he was ready to resume posse duty. Within a few months, Ben was working on longer forages that required longer periods of absence from home, once again. To return home after two dangerous weeks in the untamed western lands and discover a second betrayal was more than Ben could take.

Bass remembered when his son had confided to him only a few months before about his wife's infidelity. When asked what he would do, Bass said Ben should have tracked down the transient, threatened him with his life, and then chased him out of the Indian Nation. The memory of this private conversation drummed through Bass. He remembered the violent and uncontrollable rage that had roared through him as a young man when he slugged Master George so many decades before.

No marshal or deputy marshal who worked for the court wanted or dared to serve the writ to Ben Reeves.

Marshal Bennet was assigned to deal with the onerous and awkward task. He hesitated to send a lawman after the son of his most loyal and skilled deputy and the writ had been delayed a few days, to be dealt with when Bass returned. He was not surprised when Bass stormed into his office early the next morning vehemently insisting that he be given the warrant to serve his own son, now a wanted criminal in the Indian Nation. Marshal Bennet knew better than to argue with Bass and handed him the document.

Ben had fled to the wild hinterlands of the Indian Nation andMarshal Bennet knew that no one knew that territory better than Bass Reeves. Bass grabbed the writ and stuffed it deep in his vest pocket. He had strong inklings of where Ben was probably hiding out. Dark thoughts circled through Bass and he continued to wonder if he was in some way to blame for his son's criminal act. *Was he to blame for what happened when Ben found Lucile again with a new lover only weeks later? What had happened to the adulterer?* He was thankful that Jennie had not lived to see this moment. Ben was Bass's oldest son, the first of the ten children, and held a special place in Bass's heart. To turn in his own beloved son, charged with murder, was a weight he had never expected to carry.

Only the shrill shrieks of the hawks, swooping and gliding above, interrupted Bass's morose contemplations. A tip from the Kickapoo community confirmed that Ben was hiding in the protection of a Creek family further north. He continued to mull over the difficult task ahead of him as he followed the paths and trails he knew so well.

When he saw the small log cabin where his son took refuge, Bass dismounted and walked briskly toward Ben who was stacking wood on the front porch. A wave of relief overcame both as they hugged each other. No words or explanations were necessary as Ben prepared to leave with his father. Bass delivered his handcuffed son to Marshal Bennet a week after having volunteered to bring him in. Ben had surrendered meekly, without a fight, as Bass knew he would if he served the writ. Ben told his father that the man with Lucile had escaped the moment he opened the door in a mad dash for his life.

Ben was charged with homicide and, at the trial, confessed to the crime and detailed the events of the evening. He did not defend himself and admitted with heartfelt remorse that an uncontrollable rage had overwhelmed him, and that regret about his crime, fear of prison, and mad confusion propelled him across Hell's Border to the Territories. He was sentenced to serve ten years in Leavenworth Prison, in northeastern Kansas, on the western banks of the Missouri River. Bass accompanied him to the train depot and, with great sorrowfulness, turned him in to serve his time. Ben had not been sent to the infamous gallows and, for that, Bass was deeply grateful. Cooperative and resigned to his fate, Ben was a model prisoner and well-liked by both guards and other prisoners. Ben did not abuse the bias he benefitted from as the son of the renowned and much respected Deputy Marshal Bass Reeves.

Although Ben was sentenced to serve years in prison, the townspeople, friends, colleagues, and allies of Bass petitioned for his early release. The signers of the petition felt that the circumstances of the crime of passion merited exoneration and compassion. Ben was well-liked and known as an honest man. Many of the signatories of the petition may have felt that Lucile deserved her fate, but courtesy prevailed. After all, she had been Bass's daughter-in-law, and her death at the hands of his son must have added an unimaginable shock for Bass. That Ben was the son of Deputy Marshal Bass Reeves, who had brought in some of the most dangerous outlaws in the Territories, convinced more people to sign the petition asking the court for forgiveness and leniency.

The unofficial campaign to support the Reeves family was something Bass had never expected or encouraged, and Bass was grateful beyond words to his community. The petition was successful and Ben was pardoned and released after having served less than a year. He settled in Muskogee, opened a small but prosperous general store, bought a small farm, eventually remarried, and never had a run-in with the law again.

Chapter 14

The Sun Sets on the Indian Nation

As the competition for land and the desire for statehood by the white majority gained ever more traction and enthusiasm, the increasing presence of white settlers, many of whom never questioned their rights or presumed superiority to both the indigenous peoples and the African American population, sparked racial tensions. The flourishing economic prosperity and successful businesses of many African Americans added to increased tensions among envious white settlers. Nor did the new arrivals, who had never experienced the trials and dangers of living in the Indian Nation or the Oklahoma Territories, understand the fluidity of the social dynamics among the Native Americans, African Americans, European hunters, French trappers, and transients flowing through the Indian Nation that had evolved in the past decades.

Marshal Bennet understood the increased danger an African-American lawman faced with the rapidly changing demographic of pre-state Oklahoma, but Bass never shirked from his duty to serve the law and continued to carry out arrests of whites, blacks, and tribal members without bias or favor to anyone. The oath he had taken so many decades before remained his guiding star.

Deputy Marshall Reeves did not flinch when he was sent on assignment to find and bring in the craven murderers that had killed an interracial couple near the Verdigris River north of Muskogee. The couple, Samuel and Clara (Birdie, to Samuel) Quincy, lived on a small acreage bordering the river. They had lived in the area for two decades and were not known to have ever caused trouble. They were helpful neighbors but mostly kept to themselves, growing vegetables from a wide garden plot, and selling the fruit from the small orchard they had planted a decade before. Their lives were no more hardscrabble than many of the other families in the Territories trying to survive. Samuel was born a slave in the state of Georgia. After a severe beating for inadvertently witnessing the assault of his young sister in his mid-teens, he escaped with her from the cotton plantation where he lived and fled to the Indian Nation. Healthy, young, and alert, they made the potentially fatal journey safely. Clara, the daughter of an itinerant Presbyterian missionary family traveling through the Indian Nation on their way north to the vast and dangerous Dakota Territory, was also a run-away. From the moment Samuel found her stumbling alone in the woods so many years before, he never questioned his promise to help and protect her. Her lithe movements, small delicate frame, the way she chattered nervously, and her rapid flickering hand gestures reminded Samuel of twittering sparrows and he affectionately renamed her "Birdie". Clara and Samuel, neighborly and friendly, claimed to be married and no one doubted or cared about their legal relationship.

Why Samuel and Birdie would attract the hostile attention of transients—or residents—riding through the Muskogee area was a mystery to those who lived there and knew the peaceful couple for many years. The vigilantes had stormed the small cabin in the early morning just before dawn and fatally shot the middle-aged couple to death in their home. The sound of the multiple shots fired nearby alarmed Theo Litzinger, their elderly neighbor, who was pulling on his boots before going to milk his one cow. He reached for his old Winchester and crept to his front porch, where he crouched down behind one of the supporting posts of the small deck. Two or three people on horses, judging the number from the steady clatter of hooves pounding down the packed earth road, raced past his log house and rounded the bend, going in a southerly direction toward the heart of Muskogee.

Theo inhaled deeply trying to calm his pounding heart before walking briskly on a back trail to Samuel's cabin. He feared the worst and was not mistaken. Birdie was riddled with bullets in the narrow bed and Samuel was slumped on the floor a few feet away. His right arm twitched and Theo heard a low throaty murmur. He leaned over Samuel who was struggling to say something. Stuffing the nearest pillow, albeit bloodstained, under his head, Samuel's gasping voice named two people, and then, with a deep sucking sound, he inhaled his last breath. Theo recognized the two names. Before leaving the gruesome scene, Theo gently closed their staring eyes and covered each with one of the quilts stacked on a trunk near the bed. Mounting his horse, Theo headed straight to Muskogee to find a Lighthorse Policeman who then raced to the marshal's home to report the brutal crime.

Bass's mission was to find the killers and bring them to the marshal, dead or alive. Bass and two of his posse men rode to the Quincy home to investigate the double homicide scene. Already, frightened neighbors were whispering in small groups of two or three along the road leading to the house. When the recognizably tall figure of Deputy Marshal Reeves, accompanied by two others, galloped towards them, fear gave way to relief. The best of all the deputy marshals was assigned to the case and they were confident that, in time, the killers would be arrested and brought to justice.

While the two posse men waited outside and guarded the site, Bass searched for any traces of evidence that might lead to the capture of the killers. Birdie had been shot face down as she slept in bed. Samuel must have been alerted by some sound outside before the men barged into the cabin. It was clear to Bass that Samuel had put up a good fight and possibly disarmed one of them, as evidenced by a still-sheathed knife under the upturned table. Chairs were overturned, a curtain pulled down and a small cupboard rested on its side. Shattered dishes and glassware littered the floor of the kitchen. Aside from the Bowie knife, Bass could find no other weapons or cash anywhere in the house. It was obvious to him that the killers had robbed the meager household of anything of value after the crime was committed. Bass sifted through the shards of broken pottery and found a couple of silver dollars that might have held company with other coins in a bowl or pot. Bass concluded from the rust-colored partial handprint on the edge of a knocked-over pine table and a knotted-up bloodied kerchief flung under the stove, that one of the killers had surely cut his hand badly while breaking and ransacking the pottery searching for hidden cash. He pocketed the Bowie knife, a few stray bullets, and the kerchief. Marshal Bennet might need the examples of evidence in a future trial.

Theo was outside waiting with Bass's men when Bass came out. He described the event and told Bass he surmised that two or three men were in on the brutal killing. Calling Bass aside, he told him the two names that Samuel had sputtered out before he died. Theo knew of the two men, Arlo and Cody Hendricks, twin brothers who lived alone in the woods a few miles away. Although they were recognized by most in the area, few knew anything about them. The Hendricks boys were unfriendly and refused all gestures of neighborliness. Strangers to the community, and rude to anyone who encountered them, they were regarded with distrust and suspicion. They had moved to the Muskogee area from Kentucky less than six months before, and it was rumored that they were probably on the run and hiding out from the law. It was best to avoid them and not ask questions, was the common consensus among neighbors. Only the local blacksmith, Marcel St. Clair, son of a French fur trader, who also managed a small hardtack and general store, had dealt with them when he reshod their horses and sold them two axes and a few pounds of nails. He reported that both men were rude, surly, and impatient. When the blacksmith's Kickapoo wife came from the back of the shop to tell her husband something, they did not greet her. Their stone-cold eyes frightened her and she quickly retreated to the hardware counter in the back of the business. Feeling anxious, Marcel hurried along with the task at hand.

While the brothers waited for the horses to be shod, they stood on the corner of the narrow porch, arms folded tightly across their chests, as they observed the diverse population of Muskogee going about their daily business. When they gathered up their purchases and slung the saddles back on their horse, both men glared at a young couple waiting patiently to have two horses reshod. They spoke roughly to the young black man and his Creek wife and angrily muttered something incomprehensible to the alarmed blacksmith. Heaving themselves into their saddles, they yelled out another insult and galloped off, jamming their spurs into their horses. Later, Marcel's wife told him that the two men were cursed and filled with evil intent. Marcel nodded and added an extra padlock to the door to the shop at the end of the day.

With their identity now known to Bass, he plotted how to arrest the murdering brothers without stirring up more trouble. Interracial couples and families were not uncommon, and Bass feared the intolerant and murderous brothers would target other families. He considered various artful disguises that would allow him to close in on his prey without alerting them of his plan to entrap them. *Circuit rider preacher? A peddler selling hardware and small tools? A farmer who needed help with a mired wagon? An injured trapper who needed immediate medical attention?*

Bass recognized his advantage. While most people in the area were familiar with Bass and could identify his tall silhouette from a distance, these two criminals would not. Nor was it likely they would suspect or know he was a lawman or a skilled marksman. Bass hummed quietly as he rode back to Marshal Bennet to discuss the options, and the posse men who would be his back-up should he need help.

Bass discarded the idea of being a circuit preacher. It was unlikely the two culprits would be receptive to a crusader with a Bible in hand coming to knock at their door, and there would be no way to lure them away from the cabin. A circuit preacher generally traveled alone, had no family, and was a sitting duck for any godless miscreant because his dead body could easily be disposed of without anyone ever reporting him missing.

After careful consideration of the disadvantages or merits of each possible ruse, Bass concluded that playing the role of an injured farmer with a small hay wagon snagged on a fallen log would be the most plausible deception. The rickety hay cart stored in Marshal Bennet's barn would do. He piled it with hay and a few burlap sacks of potatoes and, with the help of Abigail's fine seamstress skills, fashioned a pair of baggy and patched pants, a raggedy wool shirt, a long vest, and a straw hat. Bass shredded a few inches of the hat brim and rubbed it with mud. A thin and flimsy kerchief, faded from years of use, completed his disguise. A couple of sacks of sweet potatoes were flung on top of the hay. A chain and a padlock were stashed in another burlap bag in the corner of the wagon under a sloppily constructed bale. A broken right arm would add to his appearance of vulnerability and he tied an old wool scarf into a sling to support his arm. He was ready. Two Colt .45s were buried in the deep pockets of his tattered vest. The warrant for the arrest was folded in his shirt pocket. He attached one of Jackson's old mares to the cart. An excellent and healthy horse such as Flint would raise suspicion. As he headed north of the town, and then turned to follow the worn-down trail that was barely wide enough for the small wagon, Bass softly sang his favorite tunes. Minewa and Otis had already scoped out the area and Bass looked for the creek ahead. At the preplanned site, Bass removed the reins from the old mare and tied her to a tree where she happily nuzzled the grass and lapped at the creek water. After tossing the burlap bag with the padlock and chain under a scrabble of brush, he jammed a thick fallen branch into the wheel spokes and loosened another wheel. The rickety, wedged wagon wobbled convincingly and Bass gave it an extra push, tipping it enough to cause everything to slide to one side and causing some hay to spill on the ground. Bass had to smile at the realistic and convincing scene. Otis and Minewa were well hidden and Bass saw no trace of them, though he knew they were concealed in the brush that banked the creek. His low whistle was a signal to Minewa and Otis that he was headed on foot to the cabin to ask for help from the brothers. Letting his right shoulder sag and his hand drift limply downwards, Bass walked slowly, stopping every now and then to adjust the slipping sling… a precaution in case the brothers were watching him. When he arrived at the ramshackle cabin, he yelled a greeting and waited, slumped and leaning against a cottonwood tree. In a few moments, the brothers threw open the door and stared at Bass. The pearly handles of holstered pistols at their sides winked in the sunlight. When Bass told the two men he needed help with his tumbled and mired hay wagon near the creek, they snickered and agreed he certainly needed help. Bass paused before explaining that his elderly wife, who was with him, was unable to help him and was counting on the goodwill of neighbors.

The brothers guffawed again and, after exchanging a quick glance, agreed to check out the accident. Diversions did not come their way very often and maybe the twins could turn the situation into an entertaining afternoon. *An old black man with a broken arm in a sling and a lame wife on a remote path several miles from any town, would be fair game. Maybe the horse or the wagon would be useful. There might be some tools or even a weapon or two in the wagon. It was worth checking out.*

Now ready to play a cruel and brutal game, the brothers nodded and told Bass to hold on another minute. When they came back out of the house, a heavy hemp rope was looped around one brother's left shoulder, and a Bowie knife was attached to the thick belt of the second brother. Bass innocently commented that a heavy rope to pull the wagon upright was exactly what was needed. The brothers grinned. Yes, a long, strong rope was essential. Bass shifted his sling, grimaced as if in pain, and rubbed his limp hand. He started walking back down the path toward the creek, thanking the men for their help. *Good to know that neighbors would help each other when in trouble* he added, before quoting from the Bible and stumbling over a small exposed root.

As Bass had hoped, his measured pace was too slow and his constant pointless chatter, interspersed with Biblical references, irritated the brothers, who quickly passed him, charging ahead toward the creek. Bass turned his head as if to sneeze and gave a long low whistle alerting Minewa and Otis that company was on the way. A shadow of a smile crossed his face when he heard the loud and throaty croak of a bullfrog immediately following his whistle.

The brothers had already ransacked the wagon when Bass caught up. Loose hay was scattered and the potatoes had rolled out of the burlap sacks. The old wife was not there and they assumed she had hobbled off into the woods at the sound of their approach. *No matter, we'll get her later*, the boys agreed. They had removed the limb from the broken spokes, righted the wagon and one brother was tightening the loosened wheel. The other brother, head leaning back, scanned the trees, searching for a high thick limb to loop the rope over. Oblivious to danger and dismissive of the old man, the brothers ignored Bass when he showed up. With one brother stretched out on the ground under the cart and the other gazing at the tall elms as he looked for a stout limb, the brothers had no chance. Bass let the loose sling slide to the ground and, whipping out both pistols, he fired, winging both simultaneously. As if from nowhere, Otis and Minewa leaped out of the brush and disarmed the murderers who thrashed around on the ground. Bass handed his assistants the rope and they bound the two brothers back to back together, wrapping the tail of the rope around their heaving chests. With a serious and solemn expression, Bass turned to the captives and, before serving the writ charging them with theft and the double homicide of Samuel and Clara Quincy, he nodded at his captives and agreed that, *yes, they had been right; a thick and long rope was exactly what was needed.* If others were involved in the crime, Bass assured them, Marshal Bennet was not to be toyed with. His remarkable skills in ferreting out information that would lead to the just conviction of all were well known.

They hauled the bundled felons into the uprighted cart and thanked the brothers for repairing the wheel. As extra insurance, Otis wrapped the chain around them and padlocked the chain to the cart. Otis and Minewa rode alongside the wagon and the lawmen and his accomplices congratulated each other on yet another successful apprehension. They had diminished the criminal population of the Territories with the ambush and capture of two more homicidal and violent men. Muskogee residents and neighboring communities would breathe easier. Marshal Bennet would be pleased and, in no time, the villains would be housed in the infamous jail before facing the successor to Judge Parker, Judge Rogers.

Chapter 15

Statehood: The Birth of Oklahoma

The Indian Territories, which by treaties belonged to the Five Civilized Tribes plus other smaller tribes, did not qualify as land to be homesteaded. It wasn't until 1889 that the Unassigned Lands of the Oklahoma Territory was opened by the federal government for homesteading.

By 1876, the old Indian Nation was bordered on all sides by states of the Union. The great stampede of pioneers and settlers into the vast undeveloped lands had never abated and continued to swell. More and more, the stateless and lawless lands were seen as a hindrance to progress, blocking the free flow of trade and further development. The prevailing attitude was that much good land was going to waste because of misguided treaties that only benefited the indigenous people, desperadoes, murdering gangs, and thieves. The forced marches and relocations decades ago, of the tribes from states east of the Mississippi to the vast reservations of the Indian Nation, were of little interest to the settlers who now loudly pounded at the door of opportunity.

Settlers, a generation or two from those who had witnessed the relocation of the indigenous people, slipped with unconcern into the areas assigned by federal treaties to tribes who had endured unimaginable pain and loss during their forced marches from their homelands to the "Indian Lands" fifty years before. Determined pioneers continued to infiltrate the territories, believing they had a God-given right to cultivate and develop the land, recognizing the great potential the fertile red soil promised, the train transports, and also, fueled by rumors or the liquid gold, oil! Wealthy, powerful railroad and mining companies, and private investors lobbied Congress to open the Territories for settlement and development. Unable, or unwilling, to counter the pressure, Congress finally relented and opened the Unassigned Lands in the center of the Territories to non-Indian settlers in 1889. As the name suggested, the vast swath of prime farm and grazing land, having never been designated as tribal land, was free to be officially opened in a unique manner for settlement. Life in the remote undeveloped lands was harsh and dangerous. Some settlers inspired by youth or idealism, ill-prepared to cope with the loneliness, minimal infrastructure, blizzards, droughts, and lack of money to buy seed and farming equipment that necessitated long trips by horse to isolate trade posts, had little choice except to abandon or relinquish their homesteads. Incoming pioneers searched for relinquished property in the hopes that some of the initial hard work had been done. If lucky, they might find a previously homesteaded piece that already had a sod house, a good well, a corral, a creek, or a plowed acreage.

By the late 1880s, droves of settlers had already investigated the land and had their sights focused on choice claims. On April 2nd, 1889, more than fifty thousand dreamers and schemers lined up for the first of the four largest Land Runs and, when the shot was fired signaling the start of the run, galloped as fast and as far as they could to stake out their future home and farm. The early settlers had sneakily, under cover of night, already staked out their future claims and, with hidden posts and secreted barbed wire, were ready to stake out their claim. Covered wagons and ox carts followed, and those without either horse or wagon sometimes managed to hitch a ride with a family or even jump on the one train that led north from Texas to the land up for grabs. Truly destitute and desperate folk, carrying scant belongings in burlap bags, walked, or even sprinted to the free land, gratefully satisfied to settle for less-than-prime spots.

Within twenty minutes, as the first wave of settlers arrived, the town of Guthrie was laid out with markers, plotting out the layout of primary streets. Federal police tried to keep order as total and utter pandemonium reigned. Federal agents set up rough structures that served as claim-filing offices. By nightfall, ten thousand people were camped in wagons and tents in Guthrie and the surrounding area. Two days after the run, a post office was established, and the new town was named Guthrie, replacing the old name of Deer Creek, a train stop for the Southern Kansas Railway. It was hoped that Guthrie would become the territorial capital of the future state of

Oklahoma and, within months, the town was a thriving center of commerce, buildings, roads, saloons, shops, and community.

Those who continued to dodge the law by trying to settle on land still belonging to the tribes were arrested and taken to Judge Parker's court to be tried. Known as the "Sooners", arrests and trials in Arkansas did not deter them. Convinced that, in time, the federal government would welcome multitudes of homesteaders eager to build the future state, the Sooners remained resolute in their determination to settle in the Territories. Agitators, lobbying hard and relentlessly for early settlement and statehood, encouraged the would-be settlers to double down on their scouting expeditions in preparation for settlement, confident that the federal government would soon reward their efforts.

In 1890, in a long and well-calculated ploy, the federal government, under the presidency of Benjamin Harrison, decreed that The Cherokee Outlet, seven million acres of land in western Oklahoma that had been traded for rich land in Georgia decades before, could no longer be leased to graze cattle. He ordered all cattle to be removed from the Cherokee land, thus instantly wiping out the tribal economies the people depended on by providing grassland to the ranchers and cattlemen moving vast herds from Texas north to cattle yards in Kansas. After bitter discussions and dealings, the tribes sold their lands for $1.25 per acre to the federal government with the agreement that their people would not be removed once again, as had happened in the past. A year later, surveying of No Man's Land and the controversies that had long been debated, were resolved and the northernmost strip bordering Kansas was opened for prospective homesteaders. Many of those who had been squatting in the "Pan Handle" now could file a legal claim for the land they had cornered off as their homestead site. The Panhandle, or No Man's Land, was not as appealing as the land further south. Thousands of people living in tents and wagons waited impatiently in the desolate plain for the law to be turned in their favor. With the removal of the cattle a few years earlier and the resulting decimation of the tribes, they knew that the Cherokee Outlet would soon open for settlement.

The human stampede into an unimaginable future was inexorable and, in 1893, with the acquisition of six million acres, the Cherokee Strip was added to the Oklahoma Territories and opened to settlement by the federal government. One hundred thousand dreamers, including investors from Kansas and other states, eager pioneers, newly arrived immigrants, and farm families from other states, lined up for the fourth and largest land run in the Territories. Forty thousand staked homestead claims in record time.

By 1896, the old Indian Nation was on the cusp of yet more radical transformations with the closure of Judge Parker's court. The court crier's news reverberated through the Twin Territories:

"The honorable district and circuit courts of the United States for the Western District of Arkansas, having no criminal jurisdiction over the Indian Territories, are now adjourned forever."

In the course of his career, Judge Parker had tried more than thirteen thousand cases. Of those cases, eight thousand five hundred of the convicted pleaded guilty. Seventy-nine of those convicted were executed by hanging. Others sentenced to hanging died in custody, escaped, or were pardoned. Judge Parker, known as "the Hanging Judge", earned this nickname because his efficiency sometimes dictated the hanging of six at a time on the famous gallows known as the Government's Suspender. With the disbanding of the court, the gallows that had brought notoriety, fame, and fear to the town on Hell's Fringe, was destroyed. Citizens of Fort Smith in the past had eagerly joined hundreds of other blood-thirsty men for the morbid entertainment of multiple hangings of murdering desperados and rapists. It was agreed by all that innocent children and women, known for their compassion and sensitivity, should not witness the gruesome sights and sounds of the finals words spoken or last chortles of breath as the trap was released with a booming crack and the men dangled limply from the beam. These same citizens now felt the famed gallows did not appropriately reflect their moral progress, political correctness, or convey the welcoming impression to their town demanded by the changing times.

Rumors of vast oil reserves in the Territories circulated wildly, exciting investors, bankers, and businessmen. For decades, seepage of oil had been noted and, in 1859, the brother of the Cherokee Chief hit an oil pool when drilling for water. The well produced about ten barrels a day for a year before giving out. Two decades later, a businessman in New York contacted the Governor of the Choctaw Nation and proposed exploratory drilling in the Choctaw lands if enough of the territory could be included to make the investments in the search for reserves worthwhile. His proposal was accepted and the Choctaw Oil and Refining Company was established, opening the door to exploration in a vast twenty thousand square mile area. Many obstacles blocked the initial project and, though some oil was tapped, the one exploratory well was closed off when the owner died unexpectedly and investors withdrew support. More reliable investment prospects were to be found in Texas, already a state with an infrastructure and more reliable communication.

In 1897, the Nellie Johnstone No. 1 Well, the first commercially profitable well in the Territories, was drilled and, within minutes of tossing the dynamite-charged dart into the well, a thrilling gusher of liquid black gold spewed up. The well continued to produce seventy-five barrels of oil a day for two years before being temporarily capped off. Again, transport of the liquid product proved too costly in the, as-yet, undeveloped land and, it was not until two years later, when the Santa Fe Railroad came to Bartlesville that the crude oil could be marketed in Kansas.

Bass was well aware of these activities and had no doubt that the rail companies and investors, working hand in glove with powerful oil interests and cattle ranchers, would expedite statehood for the Oklahoma Territories. The black gold was of no interest or surprise to Bass who knew oil seeped through the ground and had, as long as he could recall, been used by the native people as fuel for fires. He knew, too, where seepages could be found, information that he suspected was of value but, if revealed, would surely hasten the end of the Territories. The population rapidly changed with more settlers as the legitimate and the cunning rushed to the Oklahoma Territories to stake out a plot or acreage. While racial tensions among the tribal communities, the freedmen, and the predominantly white newcomers began to flare, Bass persevered to rid the land of lawbreakers. Though the times were changing, Bass remained focused on his mission and did not relent from his ambitious efforts and the focus of his life for the preceding four decades.

In 1889, both the one hundred and seventy-mile strip of land previously known as No Man's Land and the Unassigned Lands in the center of the Twin Territories were incorporated into the Oklahoma Territories, allowing settlement for non-Indians and expanding the future state. The effort by the tribes and their formal proposal submitted to Congress to retain what remained of the old Indian Nation by dividing the Twin Territories into two separate states, Oklahoma and Sequoyah, failed. In 1907, The Indian Nation would become the forty-sixth state of the union and be named Oklahoma, a Choctaw phrase meaning "red people."

The last arrest Bass made in the Indian Territories fell on the eve of statehood. Bass, on his way to meet Minewa, was shot at while riding under a rickety wooden train trestle. Bass instantly rolled off his horse and played possum, an effective ruse he had used successfully many times before. The shooter waited for a long thirty minutes, watching for any sign of movement before approaching the body. Bass's pistols, his ever-ready Winchester rifle, hat, and boots would be valuable trophies, guaranteeing the gunman the respect he knew he deserved but never received from the thickheaded settlers and residents, or the inept lawmen. Bass was sprawled out on his side, listening carefully for a step or the crunch of a leaf or stick. The sniper, now sure that Bass was dead, glanced aside and spat a wad of chew to the ground at the same moment that Bass shot him in the thigh. It was his last blast at his last prisoner. After grabbing the would-be killer's pistol and stuffing it into a vest pocket, Bass blindfolded and roped the wounded gunslinger to his own horse and brought the captive back to the marshal. It was another close call. It would not be Bass's fate to die on the eve of statehood after having served in the Indian Nation for more than thirty years. As Bass rode back with his prisoner, he wondered how or if statehood with the merger of the old Indian Nation and the Oklahoma Territories, would change his life.

As had always been feared by the tribal nations of the old Indian Nation, the politically driven lobbyists and settlers had prevailed with statehood scheduled for November 16th, 1907. During the last two decades of the nineteenth century, the powerful forces that had been in motion for the previous five decades accelerated the relentless drive to statehood for the Indian Territories on the east and the Oklahoma Territories located on the western half of what previously had once been the Indian Nation.

The last day that Bass served as Deputy Marshal was November 16th, the day that the Indian Nations became Oklahoma, the forty-sixth state of the union. Bass had served under the authority of seven different marshals in a career spanning thirty years. The fledgling state of Oklahoma, now no longer under only federal control, fell immediately under state jurisdiction.

Prior to formalizing statehood for Oklahoma, the Jim Crow laws did not exist in the Territories. The inclusion or not of Jim Crow laws in the new state was hotly debated. Enacted in the 1880s by the South, the notorious Jim Crow Act sought to legalize racial discrimination by enforcing segregation of black and white citizens in schools, transportation, restaurants, churches, social organizations, cemeteries, theaters, or even public spaces, such as parks. President Theodore Roosevelt had threatened to veto the Oklahoma state constitution if it endorsed the Jim Crow policies or laws. Under Territorial Government, segregation of schools did not exist, nor was it much of an issue. Communal spaces, transportation, juries, businesses, and lawmen remained integrated. There was much to be done in the Territories and the skin color of the movers and shakers was of minimal import. As more and more white immigrant settlers and wealthy southern investors found their way into the Oklahoma Territories, attitudes tensed and narrowed.

As soon as the documents of the constitution passed scrutiny by the federal government, Oklahoma became the forty-sixth state of the union. Legislators decided to omit the controversial Jim Crow laws rather than risk a humiliating veto. They understood that with statehood came the right to legislate racial separation within the state, but the process would be long and require much public scrutiny.

One of the first laws enacted by the new state was to define and identify a *negro* as anyone with African ancestry, the first step in legalizing racism as a factor in determining the rights and privileges of the citizens of the new state of Oklahoma. Interracial marriages and the ministers who dared to wed the couples would now be committing felonies. Inspired by the Supreme Court case of *Plessy vs Ferguson* ten years earlier, the "separate but equal" ruling legalized the adoption of many more Jim Crow provisions and, with the enforced apartheid, the role of black citizens in the development of the new state was dramatically and thoroughly diminished.

Bass's career as a deputy marshal of the Indian Territories had come to an end. In this tragic twist of dreadful and perverse irony, the very justice that Bass Reeves has dedicated his life to enforce turned against him for the second time. *Strangely*, Bass thought, *the color of my skin determined that, at birth, I was a slave, and the new law that restricts me from continuing to serve as a federal lawman in the new state of Oklahoma is also because of the color of my skin.*

Bass pondered about the complex role the law had played in his life since his great respect for the rule of law had inspired him to become a lawman. At birth, the existing laws determined he was a slave. As a young man, Bass violated the existing law, assaulted his master, and escaped to the lawless Indian Nation where he lived for nearly a decade as a fugitive. A few years later, a civil war between the states exploded. New proclamations and laws passed by the victorious granted him freedom, allowing him to follow his own self-chosen path. And, then, in a remarkable turn of fortune, Judge Isaac Parker, famously known as "The Hanging Judge," hired Bass Reeves, one of the first African-American deputy marshals employed west of the Mississippi River. Judge Parker presided over the Court of the Western District of Arkansas and his jurisdiction encompassed all of the vast Indian Territories, an area comprising seventy-four square miles. Bass proudly accepted the formidable and grueling position of serving as a lawman for the next thirty-two years in the wild Indian Territories. Bass Reeves never disappointed Judge Parker or any of the other lawmen he worked with on assignments. Respected by the community, loyal to

Judge Isaac Parker and his marshals, and motivated by his steadfast belief in fairness and justice, Bass was an inspired choice who succeeded in bringing in more than three thousand outlaws in his three-decade-plus career. Judge Parker never regretted hiring Bass to help him rout out the desperadoes, cattle rustlers, and fugitives seeking haven in the anarchy that swirled in the lands bordering Arkansas. When the son of Deputy Marshal Bass Reeves was charged with murder, Bass served the writ, arrested him, and brought him to court. His son, convicted of the homicide, was incarcerated as the current law dictated. In time, his son was saved by a legal reversal and released.

And, now with statehood, new laws would prohibit Bass from continuing his career as a federal deputy marshal, dedicated to the mission of routing out lawbreakers and violent criminals from the land he knew so well.

Because Bass was so highly regarded and respected, he was given a police beat in the segregated and predominantly black neighborhoods of Muskogee. Prior to statehood, Muskogee was one of the most vibrant and integrated towns in the Oklahoma Territories. More than eighty of the businesses in the town were owned and managed by the black community, which also boasted eleven lawyers and ten doctors. Well-known, feared, and highly admired, Bass, now using a cane, patrolled the streets on foot with the same vigilance and dedication he had always displayed. His presence commanded such great respect that, in the two years that he served as a city police officer, no crimes were committed on his turf.

Three years after statehood, Bass Reeves died of Bright's disease, leaving a legendary legacy testified to in the many obituaries, court documentation, and numerous essays written at his death. At his death, the obituary in the Muskogee Phoenix read:

"In the history of the early days of Eastern Oklahoma, the name of Bass Reeves has a place in the front rank among those who cleansed out the old Indian Territory of outlaws and desperadoes. No story of the conflict of government officers with those outlaws, which ended only a few years ago with the rapid filling up of the territory with people, can be completed without the mention of the Negro who died yesterday. During that time, he was sent to arrest some of the most desperate characters that ever infested Indian Territory and endangered life and peace in its borders. And he got his man as often as any of the other deputies."

Numerous articles written about Bass circulated around the nation and all who had lived in the old Indian Nation affirmed the truth of the upright justice of the lawman, who had never ceased to uphold the rule of law in the wild western territory.

Epilogue

Was Bass Reeves the Lone Ranger?

The turbulent chaos that reigned during the last quarter of the nineteenth century in the Old West was no more dramatic than in the Indian Territories of pre-state Oklahoma. Emancipated slaves, war refugees, and the diverse and dehumanized Indian population of the Five Civilized Tribes tried to sustain a living, while outlaws from all states of the union hid safely in the lawless country.

Scholars and researchers have noted several dramatic parallels between Bass Reeves and the adventures and fictional character of the Lone Ranger. Passionate controversy about this continues. Though the Lone Ranger was the creation of Gaylord DuBois, Fran Stryker continued the stories and, in 1933, the Lone Ranger, a masked lawman, became a much-listened-to and wildly popular radio program. Gaylord Du Bois and Fran Stryker researched the stories of the Old West for inspiration and surely came across news articles documenting captures and escapades of Bass Reeves, and it is not at all unlikely that they modeled their hero after Bass. The many articles and commentaries about Bass Reeves, peppered through the news of those days, were available to all.

Unlike the Lone Ranger, Bass was not a Texas Ranger, but an escaped slave. Bass frequently used disguises, camouflage, and masks to approach the alleged criminals. He traveled with Indian sidekicks. He liked a light-colored horse with a white mane. He loved to pass out silver dollars, but not silver bullets, as did the fictitious Lone Ranger. Like Bass, the Lone Ranger could communicate with the tribes, had a reputation as an outstanding marksman, was ambidextrous, and was always driven by a sense of fairness and justice to rout out the desperados, thieves, and outlaws who brought such grief to the settlers and the Native American communities. Bass Reeves was often referred to as "The Masked Marshal" because, from a distance, his skin color was sometimes mistaken for a mask.

For many enthusiasts of the era of the Old West, it is very conceivable that Bass Reeves inspired the wildly popular fictionalized character who came to such tremendous radio fame. That Bass Reeves might be cast as a white man is not surprising. Racism festered in the South and thousands of men and women were murdered in brutal attacks by violent mobs. Lynchings and burning of African-Americans were prevalent in the thirties in the South, and the innocents, doomed by skin pigmentation, were strung up on trees or burned in their homes. The hanging bodies were visible to all and served as a warning to the black communities. Forty years later, Billy

Holliday's sad commentary on this travesty was the subject of her 1939 hit, Strange Fruit.

The heroic escapades of a black man in the late nineteenth century would have been unimaginable, infuriating, and even traitorous to the radio-listening audience in the South. To present the Lone Ranger as a black man with historic accomplishments would never have been accepted or believed. There was little tolerance or education that supported the true role African Americans had in the conquest and settlement of the Old West. The significant contributions of African Americans as cowboys or black lawmen were erased from popular history and the pervasive and thorough white-washing of history was not contested. Whether the controversial suggestion, disputed by some scholars and historians, is true or not, the parallels between the fictional Lone Ranger and Bass Reeves are dramtically noteworthy.

In conclusion, to quote Dr. Art Burton, leading scholar on this subject: "Bass Reeves was the most outstanding peace officer of his era. Given the historical and social context Reeves worked in, and his accomplishments in his line of endeavor, the man was a phenomenon. Bass Reeves was one of the greatest frontier heroes this country has ever produced—a true giant of the American West."

In 1992, Bass Reeves was inducted into the National Cowboy Hall of Fame (National Cowboy and Western Heritage Museum), joining the ranks of the legendary heroes of the Old West. In 2006, three paintings of famed lawmen, Quanah Parker, Bud Ledbetter, and Bass Reeves, were added to the Oklahoma State Capitol , a recognition long due. Bass Reeves is described as a former slave, federal marshal, and Muskogee police officer. A twenty-five-foot sculpture of Bass Reeves mounted on his horse and headed for the Indian Nation was commissioned in 2008 and stands in Fort Smith as a further testament to the great hero. Deputy Marshal Bass Reeves was not the only black lawman of those tumultuous times of the Indian Nation, but he was the most famous, and many think, the most dedicated to his duty of enforcing the law. Bass Reeves's life, against the backdrop of the cataclysmic time of the old Indian Nation, is celebrated annually in Muskogee, Oklahoma. In 2021, Around the World in Eighty Days, the BBC/PBS TV series, Gary Beadle was cast as Bass Reeves and appeared in a cameo scene in Episode 7. Currently there are several project in work that will feature the heroic lawman, Bass Reeves. Morgan Freeman is working on a new series, Twin Territories, while Taylor Sheridan is working on another show to be titled 1883: Bass Reeves.

In the June 2022 Hollywood newsletter, Deadline, Morgan Freeman comments "I grew up in the movies watching everything, particularly Westerns, and one of the things that really busted me up was the fact that if you were Black in one of these Westerns, you'd better be a comedian. You'd better be funny," he says. "There were no [Black] heroes, and that's not

American history at all, so here's a chance to redo that, to straighten out some of the kinks in history."

It is exhilarating to many admirers of Bass Reeves that his legacy is finally receiving the recognition long denied or ignored.

About the Author

Assunta Martin retired from teaching English to international students at Oklahoma State University in 2016. She spent a decade teaching in Japan before returning to the US. She has written articles for various academic journals and co-authored text books currently used in Japan. With retirement, she was able to continue to research this narrative which had attracted her interest many years before.